RL 4.2

The Trouble with Mothers

MARGERY FACKLAM

• ─────── •

The Trouble with Mothers...

Clarion Books | *New York*

Clarion Books
a Houghton Mifflin Company imprint
52 Vanderbilt Avenue, New York, NY 10017

Copyright © 1989 by Margery Facklam

Library of Congress
Library of Congress Cataloging-in-Publication Data
Facklam, Margery.
The trouble with mothers / Margery Facklam.
p. cm.
Summary: What is a boy to do when his teacher-mother's
historical novel is given as an example of the kind of "pornography"
that should be banned from schools and libraries?
ISBN 0-89919-773-6 : $12.95 (est.)
[1. Censorship — Fiction. 2. Mothers and sons — Fiction.]
I. Title.
PZ7.F125Tr 1989
[Fic] — dc19   88-20358
                                                CIP
                                                AC

P 10 9 8 7 6 5 4 3 2 1

For my Maggie
and her sweet Kate

With special thanks
to the real Buzzard
and his three brothers,
who also fill my life
with joy.

The
Trouble
with
Mothers

1

In English class I was drawing the last scale on a two-headed half-robot, half-Godzilla monster on my notebook when Buzz poked me. I'm going to have a permanent hole in my back before the end of the semester with him sitting behind me. I heard him say, "Luke and me, we'll take that Major guy."

I turned around. "What guy?"

Too late. There was Mrs. Lester staring down at me like one of those gargoyles on the town hall. "Fine. That's a good choice, don't you agree, Mr. Troy?"

Mr. Troy. Geez. She calls you mister when she's mad. Real quick I said, "Sure, Mrs. Lester. Right. The Major is a good choice."

She hates that. She's always trying to catch you, and she hates it when she thinks you don't know what's going on but you manage to pull it off anyway. "Fine then," she said, real stiff. "Arthur and Luke will interview Major Madison at the town hall this afternoon at two. It's in the meeting room. You'll need a pass to leave school early."

Arthur is really Buzz, and it's a long story, but basically he's called the Buzzard because that's what he looks like when he's on the starting block at a swim meet. He lifts his arms real slow and high so his bony shoulder blades stick out. And then he flaps his arms to warm up. Anyway, old lady Lester moved down the aisle to attack someone else and I whispered to Buzz. "Not bad. Skip math. But what's the big deal with this Major?"

"Who cares?" Buzz said. "Some army guy maybe. Doesn't matter."

But, boy, did it matter. After the bell rang, Buzz filled me in on what we had to do.

"Where were you, Troy? Unconscious? Didn't you get any of it? You know, for a teacher's kid you're something."

"What's that supposed to mean? My mother does her thing. I do mine. And yeah, I heard it. Some of it. I heard Lester say the interviews were for the journalism project. I just didn't get the part about why this Major's important enough for an interview."

"I don't think any of these guys are any big deal," Buzz said. "I mean, Sikorski's going to interview the manager of Pizza Hut."

We went to math last period to give Mr. Bates our pass so he wouldn't turn us in for skipping, but he had a substitute which took all the fun out of it. Then we got out of there. On Mondays we don't have swim practice because the teachers have a faculty meeting. Buzz and I are on the junior high swim team. You can't be varsity or even jv until ninth grade. We're in eighth. I swim butterfly and freestyle relay. Buzz is the distance man — also butterfly.

We took our time getting our bikes out of the rack behind school. "What are we supposed to ask this guy?" I said. "I don't even know what he does."

"Relax. Lester says it's a press conference."

"So?"

"So there'll be senior high kids there interviewing him for their paper, and maybe even some real reporters. They won't pay any attention to us, and we'll just write down the stuff the guy tells them."

We didn't exactly speed to get to the town hall. And we didn't exactly take the direct route either. The town hall is half old and half new, kind of like the town. The old half looks like a grungy castle with a couple of turrets. The new red brick wing they stuck on the back is the jail and courthouse. The meeting room's in the basement of the castle part.

It was packed. A guy carrying a video camera on his shoulder moved over when we pushed open the door. "Couple seats in front," he told us.

Standing in the back was fine with me, but no chance. A bony lady with fingernails like claws grabbed my arm. "Come in, boys. You're late. See those two seats in the front row?" she hissed. There wasn't much we could do but sit in them.

Buzz was right. A bunch of senior high kids were there and the weekly *Herald* had sent over a guy who sells ads. If this was a press conference, big deal. I don't know how much we'd missed, but it sounded like the Major was winding down. He clapped his hands and rubbed them together, and paced back and forth a couple of times, shining his big smile around.

"Well now, I'm sure you have some questions. A good-looking group of young people like you must have things you'd like to ask me."

He didn't look like any kind of major I'd ever seen. He was short and kind of pudgy, but he looked neat in a suit that sure wasn't any Sears catalog special. He had wavy white hair and eyes that looked too blue to be real. Contacts, I thought, but later when he took out his glasses to read something, I knew the blue was all his own. The voice sounded too good to be real, too, deep and rolling like he'd taken lessons. But even so, there was something about the way he looked right at you that made you listen.

"Don't be shy," he boomed. "Now that you've heard my reasons for bringing our Crusade to your town, you may be interested in my first feeble efforts as an author. Any questions?" He held up a book. Two rings he wore on one hand flashed in the light. I poked Buzz. He pretended to gag.

The Major chuckled, but you got the message that he didn't really think his book was any feeble effort. "Well, perhaps you've not had a chance to read it yet. So, tell me about yourselves. I've been told we have some budding authors in the audience. That's just fine, real fine. Speak up. Let's see who you are."

A skinny girl in the front row raised her hand and mumbled something about a novel she wanted to write. I tuned her out. "What are we supposed to write about this guy? What's this crusade thing?" I whispered to Buzz.

Suddenly I felt the Major looming over me and the room was quiet. It was real hear-a-pin-drop time. Talk about being the center of attention.

"Ah, yes," the Major said like he'd found a target. "And can you share that thought with us, young man?"

The room felt like a sweaty armpit. Why didn't someone open a window? I swallowed a couple of times before I managed to croak out, "Yes sir, Mr. Major. I was just asking my friend here, um, if he caught, um, yeah, the name of the book you wrote."

The Major beamed like a toothpaste ad. "My, my, kind of you to ask." He held the book right up to the video camera. "*The Cleaning of America* is my book's theme and title. But before I describe it further, I'd like to explain that I'm not a major as in the armed forces. No sir, Major is my Christian name, given to me by my blessed parents, God rest their souls. Major Madison, and it is a name that has served me well."

I relaxed. I was off the hook. I figured as long as he was talking about himself he wouldn't bother me. But he threw me a curve. "Are you a writer, young man? Have you come to this meeting to write an article about it?"

"No sir, I mean yes sir, I've come to write about it but no, I'm not a writer." Man, that was dumb. I got all hot again.

Good old Buzz came to the rescue. "His mother's a writer," he announced. You could hear chairs scraping and people shifting to get a look at us.

"Well now, how interesting," said the Major. "And what does she write?" You could tell he was being polite and that he didn't really care about my mother.

"Romance stories," Buzz told him, but he turned to me. "What's the name of your mom's book, *The Passionate* what?"

Major Madison froze. He did a kind of double take and

sidled a couple steps closer. "Yes, *The Passionate* what?" The passionate came out long and slow so it sounded sleazy.

Every room ought to have an escape system, a button you could push to shoot you down a tunnel. I took a deep breath but it came out wrong, like a sigh, like I was finally facing up to something. *"The Passionate Pirate,"* I told him.

A few kids laughed. But the Major's blue eyes were popping out of his head. "And exactly what is the book about, young man? I didn't catch your name, son."

I wanted to tell him I hadn't thrown it and I wasn't his son, but I stayed polite. "Troy. Luke Troy. My mother's name is Martha Troy."

The Major scratched his forehead and his rings flashed in the video spotlight. "I don't think I recognize that name." He frowned like he was giving it some heavy thought.

"She uses a, what's it called? Pen name, yeah, a pen name." Good old helpful Buzz. He was really getting into this. "What's her fake name, Luke?"

There was no way out. Why couldn't my mom write mysteries or cookbooks? I'd never live this down. "Antonia Tyson." I don't know why I mumbled, but it's just such a dumb name. Her publisher wants its romance writers to have fancy names, and Martha's kind of plain.

"Yeah, Antonia Tyson," Buzz announced like he was opening the Academy Award envelope. "And man, you should see her book. It's a real blouse-buster." That got a laugh, which only encouraged Buzz. "You know, there's a lady on the cover just about falling out of her blouse and this pirate is hugging her and it says something about being a lusty, provoca . . . what's the word? Yeah, provocative novel." Buzz was beaming right along with the Major.

This time the Major rubbed his hands together like he was going to dive into a real treat. "If that doesn't beat all. Why I'd like to interview your fine mother and find out about her books. Yes, I certainly would."

A lady in a tight blue dress fluttered over to the Major. "Excuse me, Major, but we really have to keep you on schedule, and perhaps you'd like to answer some questions about your own book. We know how valuable your time is." She backed off in a shuffle that made me think of a trained bear.

"Thank you kindly, dear lady." I thought the Major was going to kiss her hand. But he didn't. He answered a couple of questions about his *Cleaning of America* book and his crusade. A real politician. I tuned him out. Let Buzz get everything we'd need for this stupid report. He'd gotten us into it.

2

Buzz rode home with me. "Come on in a while," I said.

"Sure, okay." Buzz was up the back steps before I was off my bike. "Think your gram made cookies today?"

We go through the same routine all the time. Buzz always stays for dinner on Mondays because we go to Computer Club together. Well, almost always. Once when it was Gram's turn to cook, she was on one of her health kicks and he got stuck with liver loaf. Now he checks.

Buzz likes to see what's happening at our house because he says living in a normal house is dull. He means because I live with three women, four if you count the dog, Jezebel. Besides Jez, there's my mom, my grandma, and my little sister, Maggie.

Buzz is still talking about the time my mom was acting out a scene for one of her romance stories. I don't even notice things like that anymore, but it kind of jolted Buzz. We had just opened the front door into the hallway when my mom came flying down the stairway. She leaned over the carved railing and reached out her arms like she wanted to grab someone. "My darling," she sort of groaned. "Don't leave me. Please don't leave me." And then she ran back upstairs. She didn't even see us.

That was the first time Buzz knew my mother wrote books when she wasn't being a history teacher, and I think he's always hoping he'll get in on a good scene again. His mother's a tax accountant and his dad sells cars.

Maggie was the only one around that afternoon.

When Buzz saw her at the kitchen table he said, "Changed my mind. If it's Maggie's turn to cook, I'll see you later."

"It's a salt map. Alaska," Maggie announced, poking the thing she was making on the table. She wiped a glob of goop off her arm and gave us her famous look. She's only seven and she's perfected it already. Females have this look they give you when they think you ought to know what they're thinking. It's like a secret code. The only problem is you never know what message you're supposed to get.

"Alaska? Why purple?" I asked her. "Maggot, you're a mess. Does Mom know you're messing around?" I can't remember being such a dip when I was seven.

Maggie opened her mouth to holler, but Gram saved the day when she came into the kitchen. One glance at Maggie and she gushed. "It's beautiful, honey. And you, Luke, leave her alone." Gram would say Maggie was perfect if the kid had two heads, and I knew enough to change the subject.

"What's for dinner? Who cooks tonight?" Mom keeps

the schedule on the bulletin board, but it's under about six inches of Maggie's school papers.

"Excuse me." Gram nudged Buzz away from a cupboard so she could open it. "I've traded with your mother because I have a date. She had to stay after school for a faculty meeting, so I imagine she'll pick up a pizza."

Buzz did his Groucho Marx eyebrow flip and I knew he'd stay.

"Where're you going?" I asked Gram. She's hardly ever home. Grandpa died a couple of years ago, and Gram moped around like she wanted to die, too. But since we moved in with her, she's on her new plan. She calls it living with a capital *L*.

"Potluck supper. Roller skating after that, and if my date comes while I'm dressing, tell him to wait in the living room." She grabbed a bag of potato chips and stuck them in a basket.

"Potluck? And you're taking potato chips?"

She straightened up and looked me right in the eye. She's not very tall. "My dear, it's not what you eat, but who you eat it with that counts. By the time Esther Miller and Hannah Bradley get their salads tossed, I'll have my chip and dip on the table right next to Art Hastings. They'll never learn." Gram reached out to pinch my cheek, but I ducked.

I tossed my bookbag on a chair and opened the refrigerator. "Anything to eat?"

"Cookies in the jar," Gram said. "Kool-Aid in the pitcher."

"Kool-Aid. Yuck."

"That's it. Don't take too many cookies. You'll spoil your dinner." Gram gave us a last shot on her way upstairs.

Buzz and I each grabbed a handful of cookies and a couple of bananas, and went up the back stairway to my bedroom. This house is ancient. My great-grandparents lived here a zillion years ago, and then Grandpa and Grandma did. After my dad left us, we moved in with Gram when Mom got a job teaching at the high school.

Jez was sprawled on my bed, snoring. She opened one eye and thumped her tail. She's a plain doughnut kind of dog, just tan with no decoration. I hollered at her to get off the bed. It's the same every day. Mom's rule is no dogs on beds, so Jez gets off when someone hassles her. She jumped to the floor and I hugged her.

Buzz wandered around my room poking and picking up stuff. "You're weird, you know that, Troy? I mean look at this junk. Who in heck has a room like this? Fossils all lined up and labeled like a museum. Do you glue your rocket models to keep them straight on the shelf?" He started to mess with my stereo.

"Leave it alone," I told him.

So my room is neat. Big deal. It's organized the way I want it. The "Keep Out" sign on the door isn't kidding. You'd think living with women would mean they're always cleaning up around you. But Mom's idea of straightening up is to move her junk to another room. She files by piles, but she says she knows where everything is and not to move it or she'll get mixed up. Gram's not much better. She leaves her roller skates on the stairs, and whatever project she's doing for her senior citizen group is spread everywhere. She says I'm a throwback to Grandpa. He was an engineer, and Gram says he lived by the ruler.

"Compulsive, Troy, you're compulsive," Buzz said.

"Where'd you get that?"

"That's psychology. My mom says that to Dad all the time." Buzz flopped on the bed and Jez leaped up next to him.

I fed my guppies. "So how do we write this interview thing? You're the one who got us into this. What does Lester want?"

"Times, dates, names. You know, anything that sounds important." He pushed the dog over so he'd have room to stretch out. "You write and I'll dictate. Major Madison, author of the book, *The Cleaning of America*, was interviewed . . . no, spoke to a group of . . ."

I wrote and crossed out and wrote some more. Finally we decided on a couple of pages about how the Major was traveling to promote his book, and we put in a bunch of times and dates Buzz had copied from the kid sitting next to him at the town hall.

"Sounds good," Buzz decided. "Now let's forget that."

"Okay by me." The assignment was done, so I closed the Major out of my head. I was showing Buzz my new tapes when Maggie banged on the door.

"Mommy says you got to come down right now while the pizza's hot," she shouted.

"Okay, okay. Don't break the door. We're coming."

Mom was leaning against the wall, talking on the kitchen phone. She was still wearing her school clothes, a plaid skirt and blue sweater, but she had taken off her good shoes. She wiggled her toes and rubbed one foot on the other. She waved a "Hi" at us, then put her hand over the mouthpiece to whisper, "It's a parent. Set the table. Hello, Arthur." Then she turned her back to us. "Yes, Mrs. Winkler. Your son got the F in history because he didn't hand in any homework. Now if you'd like to make an appointment to talk with me at school, I'd be happy to. . . ."

It sounded like it was going to be a long conversation, so I shoved the high stool over to her and she sat down and mouthed the words, "Thank you."

"Grab the plates," I told Buzz. I took the pizza box into the dining room and shoved some papers to one end of the table to make room for us.

We heard Mom hang up and the refrigerator open and close. "Who wants milk?" she called.

We got that decided, and we'd already started eating when Gram sailed into the dining room. She was wearing her skating outfit, which I think is kind of short for someone her age, but Mom told me once it's none of my business. Over one shoulder Gram carried her white roller skates with the red pompoms on the laces. She bent down to give Maggie and Mom each a pat on the head and a peck on the cheek. I didn't duck in time to miss the kiss, but I didn't really mind. It's just when she pinches my cheek that I hate it.

"Don't wait up," Gram said. "There's a special speaker tonight at the dinner, so skating starts later than usual. Art's picking me up; I'll wait on the porch."

After we'd said good-bye to Gram, Mom tossed out her

standard question, "So, how was school?" Maggie took it as her cue to treat us to one of her fascinating reports. This time it was about some kid who threw up on the teacher's shoes. Mom changed the subject. "How's your mother, Buzz? I haven't seen her in ages."

"Okay, fine. She's working full time now at the bank." I could almost see wheels turning in his head, searching for something to talk about. He found it. "You writing another book, Mrs. Troy?"

"Trying." She shrugged. "I don't know, sometimes I wonder why. I don't even know if anyone's reading my first book."

Buzz lit up. "They will be, Mrs. Troy. I guarantee it. We gave it a great sales pitch today."

"Really? What brought that on?" Mom asked.

"We had to do interviews for English class," I told her.

"Ah, yes, the interviews. I saw Rita Lester at the faculty meeting. She mentioned that you aren't working as hard as you should be in English, Luther." Mom delivered that zinger with her laser-eye look. It's just great being a teacher's kid, just great. Everyone expects you to get straight A's and be Mr. Perfect.

"She also mentioned that you were starting the journalism unit. In fact, I'm going to be interviewed. Three of your girl friends are coming over tonight to talk to me."

"Girl friends?" Buzz did his Groucho Marx eyebrow flip.

"Who?" I wanted to know who she thought would be our girl friends.

"Mary Alice, and Bess, and I forget the other one."

Buzz croaked. "Haw! Muffy, Buffy, and Puke."

I kicked him under the table so he'd shut up. "Aw Mom. They're coming over here?"

"For heaven's sake, Luke. They're coming to see me, not you. Anyway, don't you have Computer Club tonight? You won't even be here."

"Yeah." Saved. I wouldn't have minded just Bess so much, but Mary Alice is a creep. The other one must be Jennifer Bates. She thinks she owns the world.

"Well, tell me about this interview you went to," Mom said. "It might help if I knew what sort of information Mrs. Lester wants you kids to find out."

"Gee, Mom, nothing special. I mean this was just some guy who's going to clean up the environment," I told her. But that's as far as I got because just then the phone rang and Jez got all riled up and started chasing her tail when Art Hastings honked in the driveway for Gram.

Mom answered the phone and I told Maggie, "Your turn to clean up."

She grumped some dumb comments, but she took the plates and stuck them in the dishwasher. I carried out the glasses and Buzz grabbed the pizza box. Mom was perched on the kitchen stool again, still on the phone with some friend of hers, when Buzz and I left for Computer Club.

I didn't get home until late. I hollered, "I'm home," but nobody answered. Maggie was probably in bed, and I figured Mom was in her favorite hangout, the bathtub. I wandered into the living room. The TV set was playing to an empty room. The news was on, and I was just going to switch it off when the Major's big face flashed on.

· 15 ·

I plopped on the couch to watch. The Major was telling the newsman about how much he loved our town and then he said, "I'm pleased that some of your concerned citizens have persuaded me to bring my Crusade for a Clean America right here. I'm also pleased to announce that Mrs. Edith Baxter has agreed to chair the local Crusade committee, and we're having our first meeting at the Grange hall on Wednesday evening at eight o'clock. I hope you'll all come and help us plan for a truly inspirational rally." He waved at the camera and his rings flashed like winking lights.

I was still staring at the screen when Mom wandered in, tying her plaid bathrobe. "Hi, honey. Did you have a good meeting?"

"Yeah. Really neat. Sikorski thinks he can break into the school computer."

Mom smiled and shook her head. "Not likely. I'd guess the principal changes the code often enough to keep anyone guessing. What's on the news? Anything exciting?"

"Nothing much. Usual stuff."

"You mean a couple of muggings, a beauty pageant, and a politician promising all that's good and perfect?"

"Yeah, that, too. You know that guy we interviewed? He was on."

"Really? What's his name? What does he do?"

"A weird guy. Flashy. His first name's Major, would you believe that? Major Madison. He's having a rally. Something about cleaning up America. I think it's one of those ecology things."

Mom froze. "Cleaning America? Are you sure?"

"Well, I didn't listen real close," I had to admit, "but I'm sure that's the name of it. He's having a meeting Wednesday. Why?"

"If it's the Major Madison I've read about, I think it's a crusade of censorship. I hope I'm wrong, but I'll bet he's here to clean out our libraries. Let's hope he doesn't go after the schools, too."

"What do you mean, go after the schools?"

"Nothing. Don't worry about it. I'm probably just borrowing trouble. The people in this town are far too intelligent to be taken in by someone like this Major," she said. "I hope. Well, it's late. Better get to bed, son."

"Okay. Good night, Mom."

A few minutes later when I was just getting into bed, Mom knocked on my door, then pushed it open a crack before I could shove Jez off the bed. "Luke, when did you say they were having a meeting for this Crusade thing?"

"Wednesday, yeah, I think that Major guy said Wednesday."

"Wednesday . . . Well, good night dear, 'night Jez," she mumbled and closed the door. I couldn't believe it. She hadn't even ordered Jez off my bed, which wasn't like Mom at all.

3

Nothing special happened until Wednesday. That was when our interview homework was due in English. Mrs. Lester is kind of like that lady in the French Revolution who counted heads rolling off the guillotine. She cruised up and down the aisles looking for her first victim. "Let's hear some of the interviews. Who'd like to go first?"

So who raised her hand? No surprise. Mary Alice. She marched up to the front of the room and flashed me her shark-tooth smile. I had to force myself to keep my foot out of the aisle.

"As you know," Mary Alice said as if she were on "Good Morning America," "Bess and Jennifer and I interviewed Antonia Tyson."

"That's really Mrs. Troy, Luke's mother," Jennifer said from the back of the room.

Mary Alice gave her a dirty look. "I was going to say that. Antonia Tyson is her nom de plume. That's French. It means pen name — a fake name." Mary Alice acted like she was queen of the world.

While she read her interview with my mom, I slid down

in my seat as far as I could go. Man, how do guys handle it? I mean what if your dad were President, or the principal or something? Mary Alice droned on about where Mom went to college and how she worked for a newspaper and when she met my dad. Then she got to the part about raising a family.

Buzz poked me in the back. "That's you," he said. Like I didn't know.

My mother must have told them everything there was to know about us. Mary Alice went all through the part about how many years Mom tried to sell one of her romance books before a publisher bought *The Passionate Pirate*. I tuned out. It seemed like Mary Alice talked for two weeks.

Finally the kids clapped and Mrs. Lester beamed. It was over. "That was just lovely, girls. You did an excellent job. And perhaps we can persuade Mrs. Troy to visit our class and tell how she wrote her book." Mrs. Lester was so excited I thought she was going to faint. But she snapped out of it. "Yes, well." She glanced at the clock. "Time for one short interview before the end of class. Does anyone have a short report? Henry? Is your interview ready?"

"Too long," Sikorski told her. "Much too long."

I stared at the floor. That's the secret. Never let her catch your eye. But she zeroed in on Buzz. "Your interview, Arthur. Let's keep this author's day. You and Luke interviewed Major Madison, if I remember correctly?"

If she remembered correctly? She's got a mind like an elephant. Buzz stalled. He's the best; he can keep a teacher dangling better than anyone. "Mmmm, gee, Mrs.

Lester. I don't know." He mumbled so she had to ask what he'd said. That was a couple seconds right there. He poked me again. "Luke, do you have the final copy of our interview? I can't seem to find it in my notebook." He dragged out every word.

That was my cue. I opened my notebook and leafed through it one page at a time, real slow and careful, like I was reading it. "Gee, I thought you had it. Remember after we finished, you said you'd copy it over so it would be real neat?"

"No, you did that. Don't you remember? You told me I always did such a messy job. And I can't spell, and. . . ."

Mrs. Lester whapped her ruler on the edge of the desk so hard I jumped a foot. "All right! That's enough. Do you or do you not have the assignment ready?"

"Yes ma'am, we do." Buzz pulled out some papers and waved them over his head just as the bell rang. "Saved by the bell," Buzz said, but not quite loud enough for Lester to hear him. He never goes too far. A real genius.

"Leave your papers on the desk," she ordered. We did, and on the way out Sikorski grabbed me.

"Hey, you guys going to the rally tonight?"

"Naw, who needs it? Bor — ring," I told him. "Anyway, there's swim practice at seven. Coach says we need extra time before the Prescott meet."

"Aw, come on," Sikorski said. "Nothing else is going on."

"Hey, why not?" Buzz said. "Yeah, after practice why not? Grange hall, right? See ya, Sikorski."

*

We were just finishing dinner that night when Gram said, "Oh, I almost forgot. The senior center made the papers."

"No kidding? What for?" Mom reached for the newspaper Gram held out.

"It's just a little notice about that speaker we had last night, a Major Madison."

"The Major? Interesting. What's he like? What did you think of him?" Mom asked.

"Well, he certainly throws the charm around and he's an entertaining speaker," Gram said. "But it was kind of scary. He wants us to throw away our dirty books and records. Now who on earth is keeping dirty books around? I ask you! Did you know he's here on what he calls a crusade? Edith Baxter is chairman."

"Edith? Well, why not? She leads everything else," Mom said.

"Are you talking about Eddie's mother?" I asked.

"Yes, dear," Gram said. "Didn't she lead the fight for planting trees along the highway last spring?"

"Yeah. That was great. But she was the one who made them serve health food in the cafeteria." Mom laughed when I said that. "It wasn't funny. And remember when she was our fourth-grade room mother? She convinced all the other mothers to cut out cupcakes and good stuff for birthday parties and snacks."

Mom was still laughing. "Oh yes, I'd forgotten. She sent home her health food recipes. But that was okay, I didn't mind. And then remember how she got everyone together to buy that terrific playground for the elementary school," Mom reminded me.

"A lady with a cause," Gram said. "Any cause at all, it seems. I'm not sure she picked a good one this time."

"Well, I guess we'll find out," Mom said. "Luke interviewed this Major Madison, you know."

"My, my." Gram looked impressed. "It may interest you to know that the Major particularly mentioned romance novels in his speech last night, Martha."

"Oh great." Mom sighed. "Did he say why he picked on romances?"

Gram shrugged. "He says they give people an unrealistic view of life."

"He didn't say anything about Mom, did he?" I asked Gram.

Mom turned and gave me one of her piercing looks. "Now why in the world would he specifically ask about me?"

"Oh, no reason. Just wondered."

Mom frowned. "Luther, when Buzz said he gave my book a sales pitch, what exactly did he mean?"

I shrugged. "I don't know."

"Did you by any chance tell this Major Madison that your mother wrote one of those romance novels?"

"Yeah, Buzz did mention that, but it wasn't really any big deal. The Major only wanted to talk about his own book."

Gram started to clear off the table. "I don't think it's anything to worry about, Martha. Your book hardly qualifies as anything to be censored. Come on, Luke, help me clean up, will you, dear?"

*

I was practically the last one in the locker room for swim practice that night. Jim Chang saw me first. "Troy," he yelled. "Hey, it's the son of romance." He held out his arms like he was grabbing a girl, and smacked the air with fat kisses.

"Yeah, Troy, how come you're so backward with the women?" someone hollered. Real comedian.

"What's with you guys?" A wadded sock sailed by me, but I ducked and it caught Chang right on the mouth.

"Gorp, yuck." Chang pretended to barf. "Keep your moldy junk out of my face." He sent a sneaker sailing and it caught another guy on the head.

"Okay you guys, can it!" Coach Huntley stuck his head in the doorway and gave us a blast on his whistle. He must wear that thing to bed. "Let's go, let's go," he screamed. "We don't have all night."

We did our practice laps and then, just when we were ready to die, old man Huntley really started the workout. The man thinks we're machines. It was 8:30 before we got out of there.

I decided to go along with Buzz, Chang, Hank Sikorski, and Eddie Baxter to see what was happening at the Grange hall. At least it would be something different. And anyway, after the conversation at dinner, I was kind of curious to find out what the Major was up to. We heard the music before we rounded the corner. Cars were parked everywhere, up and down both sides of the street and on lawns.

We pulled open the door and squeezed into the back of the main hall. A tight fit; it was standing room only. I'm kind of short, and stuck behind Eddie Baxter, I couldn't see much. Eddie's built like a flagpole, and so tall that the high school basketball coach has been following him around since sixth grade. I guess he's afraid Baxter will move before he can get him on the varsity. Fat chance. Eddie hates basketball. He's going to get a scholarship for sure for breaststroke. Man, when he's cutting through the water, he looks like one of those skinny-leg water bugs. A giant one.

Eddie groaned. "Aw no, my mother's up there on the stage. Another committee. I hate that. Nothing but microwave specials to eat until she's through with this one."

"What's happening?" I could see flags across the back of the stage, and between Eddie's shoulder and a fat man in front of us I'd get a glimpse every couple seconds of the Major pacing back and forth like a sentry. He was talking, only it sounded a lot like those television preachers, and I was glad we'd missed part of it. When I stood on my toes and craned my neck, I could see Mrs. Baxter sitting at the end of a row of folding chairs on the stage. No wonder Eddie looked like a flagpole. So did she, but more like she was built of pipe cleaners. I looked around for my mother, too, but all I could see were backs of heads.

The Major was saying, "Dear friends, I've told you of the wonderful response we've had to our Crusade across this nation. Now you have an opportunity to join us, to examine the atmosphere in which your children learn, to assure yourselves that you and your loved ones are not exposed to evil ideas, or smutty suggestive books and records and video recordings. This is not a witch hunt." He stopped for a beat, and I could see between the shoulders ahead of me that he was giving the audience a long hard look.

"This town was added to our itinerary at the request of some of your finest fellow citizens, and you are here, I am certain, because you want the best for your families, your community, your country." There were a few cheers and some clapping, but a lot of muttering. The Major raised his arms like a signal to settle down. "We would like you to go away from this meeting to spread the message. Tell your friends about the rally a week from Friday."

From way over in the corner near the front of the audience, I saw a woman stand up, a short woman. "I'd like to ask exactly what your message will mean to our freedoms, sir. In this town we are accustomed to reading whatever books we choose." I knew the voice. My mother's.

Oh great. This was just what I needed. I wanted to get out of there, and fast. I felt sorry for Baxter. At least my mother wasn't on the stage, but this was bad enough. When I pushed my way through the people who had moved in behind us, someone shoved a pamphlet into my hand. "Clean Books for a Strong America," it said. I dropped it in the trash can and headed home.

I was in bed before Mom got back from the rally, and in the rush to get to school the next morning, our only conversation was stuff like, "Do you have your lunch, Luke?" and "Maggie, you'd better take a sweater." It wasn't long, though, before the subject of the Major came up again.

4

Thursday morning all eighth graders were herded into the gym to take a whole bunch of tests. What do they do with all that junk anyway? I guess they're trying to figure out what classes to put us in for high school or if we should be lawyers or barbers or what. After they get that done, then we'll have to talk to guidance counselors, and they'll want to know what our goals are. Goals? Mine is to beat Buzz in the 100 butterfly this season. He keeps shaving off a tenth of a second and I keep coasting in the same every time. I mean, he's my best friend, but I'd trade my stereo to break his time.

We had phys. ed. right after lunch. I used the locker next to Eddie Baxter. "How'd you like the tests?" I asked, just for something to say.

"I gotta keep my mouth shut about those," he said. "My mother'd be over here with a flame thrower if she found out I answered all that stuff."

"That's crazy. Why?"

"Aw, she's all hung up on the school staying out of our private lives, you know? Remember the hygiene class in sixth grade? Man, she had them on the ropes about that. She told them it was none of their business what I knew about health. She meant sex. She wouldn't even let me read the textbook. And now she's on that committee about the books. I'm not going to hand her anything else to get hot about."

I wondered if my mom would get hot about the stuff she heard at that rally meeting last night, but if she did, I knew she sure wouldn't agree with Eddie's mom. Anyway, it wasn't my problem.

Chang had wandered in. "Listen, the secret of these tests is to give 'em what they want. Average. With just a hint of potential."

Sikorski barged in. "What're you talking about?"

"I'm telling you," Chang said, "you don't want to look weird, see, but they've got to see a spark of something. You've got to let them discover something they think you'll be great at. But you can't look too good or too dumb. Like, what answer did you put on that question about how often you wished you had different parents?"

"About once a week," I admitted.

"Naw. That's one of those clues that some guidance counselor will pick up and zap, you'll be talking to the school shrink." Chang tossed his clothes into the bottom of his locker and slammed it shut.

"You're out of your skull," Sikorski said.

"Want to bet?" Chang said. "Listen, my dad's been transferred five times I can remember, and when you've been in as many schools as I have, you've seen every test they ever wrote. I'm telling you, I got it figured. Like when they want to know your goals, you gotta make them think. . . ."

"Goals? I'll give you goals. Let's move it." Coach Huntley poked his head into the locker room and we moved.

I had just finished my shower after gym class when I heard Huntley bellow for me. "Troy. In my office. On the double." I wondered if he made his own kids do everything double time. Holy cow, now what?

"Phone for you," Huntley said.

"For me? Who is it?" No one ever gets a phone call in a class unless it's trouble.

"Just take it, Troy."

But it was only Mom. "Hi, honey. I need your help, dear." I knew that meant babysitting. "I've been asked to be on the 'Conversation with Connie' TV show, but they're taping it after school today and Maggie's having her Brownie meeting at our house. It's Gram's day to help at the soup kitchen downtown. Could you do it, dear?"

"Do what?"

"Take charge of Maggie's Brownie meeting. Please? I tried to get one of the other mothers, but everyone's busy. I wouldn't ask you, Luke, but this is a fantastic chance for me to debate this Major. He's going to be on the show, too."

I was trapped. I knew I'd have to say yes, but I tried anyway. "I don't know what to do with those kids, Mom. Can't you just cancel it?"

"Listen, Luke. I don't have time to argue. I'm calling from the high school office and I have to get back to class. No, we can't cancel because those children have bus passes to get off at our house." I could hear her sigh. "Please dear. Gram got everything ready. Snacks are in the refrigerator. You can pick up a pass to leave school half an hour early. Thanks, Luke. I owe you one." And she hung up.

Terrific. That's all the guys would have to hear. Brownie leader. Cripes. I'd rather scrub the kitchen floor, which I hated, too. But at least I didn't get that job very often because Mom actually liked to do it. She said it was great exercise.

The bus was just unloading Maggie and her clones in their Brownie uniforms when I got home. Seven-year-old females don't walk or talk like normal people. They dance and skip and scream and giggle. They're never still.

Poor Jez. That dog was scrambling to get outside, but she leaped on Maggie and me to say hello. Two of Maggie's friends screeched when Jez nudged them. "Cut it out," I told them. "You'll scare the dog."

There were six of these kids, but it seemed like sixteen. It took forever just to get them started on their dumb project. First they all had to go to the bathroom. Then a couple of them had to call their mothers at work to let them know they got to the Brownie meeting okay.

Gram had covered the dining room table with newspaper, and she left a long list telling exactly how to make Easter decorations for nursing home trays. I handed out the glue and cardboard and crayons. The kids were supposed to glue half of an empty eggshell on a hunk of cardboard, fill the egg with dirt, and plant some grass seed in it. Then they were supposed to decorate it any way they wanted, and Gram had left glitter and sequins and some other stuff on a tray.

I couldn't get through to those kids, so I grabbed a whistle from a hook in the back hall and gave it a blast. They froze. It was great. "All right. Listen up." I tried to sound like the coach. "I'm going to show you where everything is and then you're going to make these tray favors. After that you'll clean up. You'll eat. And then you'll go home!"

I went through the whole project, step by step. It was so easy I felt stupid showing them, but when I told them to get started they acted like they hadn't heard a word I'd said. What a bunch of dim bulbs! Maggie grabbed an eggshell too hard and crunched it to bits. "Luuuke," she wailed. "Help."

It went downhill from there. No wonder Gram had left two dozen of these empty eggshells. They'd be lucky to end up with one each. "Luke, help me," was all these kids could say. I was all over that table like an octopus.

"I'm hungry," one kid yelled. She had glue and sequins and grass seed on her chin.

They shrieked and giggled and hollered variations of "let's eat." I blew the whistle. This time it took two blasts to shut them up. "No food until you clean up. That's an order!"

They went into a flurry of shoving stuff around. One kid passed the wastebasket, but more scraps and potting soil went under the table than into the basket. I couldn't stand to watch, so I went to get the snacks. Jez was howling on the back porch but I didn't dare let her in. The phone rang while I was pouring the Kool-Aid and by the time I got to it, the caller had hung up.

Maggie's friend, Wendy, had followed me into the kitchen. "I'll carry the drinks," she announced. Before I could stop her, she had grabbed the tray, swung around, and collided with another Brownie. Pink Kool-Aid flew around the room like a shower of fireworks. I saw it in slow motion, even though it took a split second to splatter the floor, the kids, the cupboards, everything.

Wendy screamed, the other kid screamed, I screamed, and all the other Brownies ran in to see what had happened. They skidded in the spilled Kool-Aid and tromped it back into the dining room.

"Everybody OUT," I shouted. "NOW." I opened the back door to shove them all out on the porch, but instead the dog galloped in, slid on the Kool-Aid, bumped into the table, and knocked the cupcakes to the floor. When I grabbed for Jez I stepped smack in the middle of a chocolate cupcake. Sticky white frosting oozed up the sides of my sneaker. I wanted to cry or swear.

When Mom got home I was on my hands and knees scrubbing the kitchen floor. "Why are the girls sitting on the porch steps? What's going on here?" Mom had started talking before she even saw me.

"Don't speak to me," I warned her.

"What on earth happened? Did you have trouble?"

"Trouble? That's good, Mom. Really good." I stared at her. "As far as I'm concerned, the deal's off."

"What deal? Luther, get off your knees and tell me what you're talking about."

I threw the scrub brush into the bucket. Suds splashed on the wall. "All of this. Babysitting and housework. All of it!"

I was really warming up. "Maggie's your kid, you take care of her. I've had it. You're off doing your thing, and you expect everyone else to handle what you don't have time for. Well, count me out. You're always telling me I'm the man in the family. Nuts, I'm just the maid!"

Mom's face went as blank as an empty billboard, but then her eyes got dark as a tiger's. And real low so that I could hardly hear it she said, "Why you're just like your father. I never realized that. He could only see his side of things, too." She yanked off her coat and tossed it on a chair. "Go to your room. I'll finish here."

"Fine with me. You can have it."

I didn't come out of my room until Gram called me for dinner. And that was grim. Gram tried to get a conversation going. "We had a hundred and ten people at the center today for lunch. Good soup, too. And the Kilmer bakery sent over some day-old pies, which were delicious."

"That's nice." Mom sounded like a robot. She didn't look at me, and I didn't look at her. Even Maggie kept her eyes on the design she was making with her peas and potatoes.

"So, how did your Brownie project go, Maggie?" Gram asked.

"Don't ask," Mom warned her.

Gram shot a look from Mom to me to Maggie. "That bad? Hmm, I wondered why the chilly atmosphere, also the crunch of potting soil and eggshells under the table. Okay, we'll change the subject. What time is your interview on the Connie show, Martha?"

Mom glanced at her watch and jumped up. "Oh, gosh, in two minutes. I mean the whole show is on tomorrow, but the news is doing a teaser."

"What on earth is a teaser?" I was glad Gram asked because I wanted to know, but I wasn't speaking to my mother.

"They use a couple of minutes of the most tantalizing bits, a kind of preview to make you want to watch the whole thing." Mom switched on the television.

We sat through a murder investigation and two accidents before the newsman said, "And next, a hot debate between the author of *The Passionate Pirate* and the man who says the book should not be allowed in the high school."

"Holy cow, what happened, Mom?" I said it before I remembered I wasn't speaking to her.

We moved closer to the television set so we wouldn't miss anything. Maggie started to talk, but Gram hushed her. "Not now, honey."

The commercial ended and there was a closeup of Mom. She looked terrific, not at all nervous. The announcer was saying, "Martha Troy, who teaches history at the senior high school, is also Antonia Tyson, author of the controversial book, *The Passionate Pirate*."

"Controversial?" Gram muttered. "When did it get to be that?"

They flashed to a full-screen closeup of Major Madison

and the announcer said, "Major Madison, director of the Crusade for a Clean America, today charged author Tyson with corrupting students by using her book in her history classes. Tune in at ten o'clock tomorrow morning for the full debate on this important issue."

Mom switched off the TV. The only sound was Jez's tail thumping the floor. I don't know what Mom and Gram were thinking, but the first thing that flashed into my head was how embarrassed I was going to be with everyone in town talking about us. Then real quick I thought, poor Mom. And then I thought, what the heck did she mean I only saw one side like my father?

Gram jumped up and patted Mom on the shoulder. "You look wonderful on television, dear. Cheer up. They always exaggerate the issues on those teaser things. And who watches that Connie person's show anyway?"

But even Gram's words didn't put a smile on Mom's face.

5

I was glad the "Conversation with Connie" show was on at ten so I wouldn't have to see it. We have science at ten. But wouldn't you know, Mrs. Lester taped it so we could see it in English. I hope I never spend another period like that as long as I live. It ranks right up there with having a tooth drilled without Novocain or taking dancing lessons with a girl two feet taller than me.

"Way to go, Troy," Sikorski hollered when my mother was introduced on TV. Mrs. Lester squashed him with a look.

Mom was great. She was wearing her good blue suit, and she looked real comfortable sitting there on one side of this Connie lady, who had shiny teeth, and big glittery earrings, and hair so stiff it wouldn't have moved in a tornado. The Major looked too cheerful to be real. After the introduction, Mom got to answer the first question.

"Tell us, Mrs. Troy, or shall I call you Ms. Tyson?" Connie gushed. When Mom said Mrs. Troy would be fine, Connie said, "Well then, tell us how you came to write this book."

So Mom did. "I'm a history teacher, as you know, and

when I was doing my research for my master's thesis, I came across references to a pirate who lived during the Civil War. He fascinated me."

"I would guess he did, my dear." Connie chuckled and batted her eyelashes. "Now, I know you have a family and a full-time job. Can you tell us where you find the time to write?"

"Well, it isn't easy," Mom said. "I worked on the book in my spare time and during the summer for more than three years. I'm lucky to have children and a mother who willingly share the work. They really make it possible." I slid down in my seat.

The camera moved to Major Madison who was shifting in his chair like he had an itch. He leaned toward Connie. "Excuse me, ma'am. Mrs. Troy's work habits are fascinating, of course, but I wonder if I might ask a question at this point?" He didn't wait for Connie to say okay. He went right on. "I'm wondering why anyone would waste all those precious years working on a piece of trash."

Mom looked like she'd been slapped, and even Connie gasped. That didn't stop the Major. "What I mean is, there are so many worthwhile things to write about, why would you put your energies into a lurid, unrealistic tale that gives our youngsters an exaggerated view of life? I understand your history class is using it as a textbook right now. Have you stopped to think of the wrong values you are teaching children?"

Connie spluttered, but it was Mom who stopped him. "Now just a minute, Mr. Madison. Have you read my book?" When he didn't answer, Mom kept at him. "I thought not. But whether you know anything about *The Passionate Pirate* or not, you have no right to dictate what a person may or may not read. You have no right to be a censor for anyone but yourself. And the students who are reading my book are not children. They are seniors, some old enough to vote and go to war, all old enough to see R-rated movies. What I'm saying is they are old enough to learn to make choices, educated choices. My book is not a textbook, but it does give my students some background on the slave ships that. . . ."

"Go for it, Mom." I meant to whisper but it came out louder. Some of the kids clapped. Mrs. Lester told us to hush, but she was smiling.

The Major took another shot. "My dear madam, of course you may read — and write — whatever pleases your taste, but you do not have a right to project your tastes into young, unformed minds. I do not doubt that you can come up with some sort of explanation for what I understand is a detailed rape scene in your book, but whatever that explanation is, it will not satisfy those of us who hold ourselves to higher moral teachings."

Mom tried to say something, but the Major held up his hand and kept right on. "For that reason, we have prepared a petition to the school board demanding the removal of your book from your classroom, along with a list of other questionable books that should be removed from the school library." The Major sat back looking satisfied with himself.

At that point the program broke to a commercial for toilet tissue. Mrs. Lester fast-forwarded the tape, and started it again with Connie asking a question. I can't remember all the rest of the program, but it was more of Major Madison accusing my mother of writing and promoting dirty books, and Mom trying to explain about her book and why she used it in her class. The longer the discussion went on, the more grim my mother looked.

When the bell rang at the end of the period it was like an electric shock jolting me back to the classroom. Over the scraping of chairs, Mrs. Lester called, "We'll talk about this on Monday. Have a good weekend."

Buzz walked out with me. "Hey, your mother did okay. I mean she can really hold her own."

I nodded, but I didn't feel like talking. Chang caught up with us, but Buzz told him, "Not now. Me and Troy got some private business."

Chang looked surprised. "Yeah, well, see you at the swim meet."

The halls are always packed between classes, but I hardly noticed. "What private business?" I asked Buzz.

"Hmm? Oh, nothing special. Just thought you might want to be left alone, that's all."

"Yeah. Thanks. Wish I could cut out now. Skip the rest of the day."

"Why not? Do it," Buzz said.

"Oh sure. Easy for you to say. Maybe you could figure a way, but I. . . ." I broke it off. There was no use trying to explain to Buzz. Cutting wasn't worth being grounded for a week, but even that wouldn't be as bad as sitting through Mom's lecture about honor and all that junk. I did really want to be alone for a while to sort things out.

While Mom was talking on the TV show, it dawned on me that I didn't even know it had taken her three years to write that book. And now here's this guy telling her it's trash.

"Hey, Troy, are you conscious?" Buzz punched my arm.

"What?"

"Room 114, history class. Wars, taxes, that stuff, remember?" Buzz said. "Are you okay?"

"Oh yeah, I'm okay," I told him. "Yeah, just great."

6

I remembered to take ear plugs and dry socks to the swim meet. Socks always get soaked in the locker room. It was a home meet. I liked that. There wouldn't be any surprises in our own pool. The other team's buses weren't there yet so I knew we'd have time for a good warm-up.

Buzz was in the coach's office. I heard the coach tell him, "Keep it calm. No strain. We can take Prescott if you guys stay loose."

The chlorine smell is the first thing that hits you when you push open the locker room door. And the heat, and guys yelling. But this time it was quiet. Everyone was huddled around one of the benches listening to one guy reading out loud. I knew he was reading because no one would talk like that.

"He touched her, gently at first, a soft caress. She pulled away, but he reached for her, pulled her to him and pressed her firmly against him. She gasped."

Another kid grabbed the book. "Naw. That's just mushy. It's not the good part. Page 231. That's the rape scene. I marked it. Listen to this."

"Hey, what're you doing?" I asked.

Sikorski was the first one to break away. He looked embarrassed when he saw me. "Come on, guys. Coach's gonna be madder than hell. Let's go."

The bunch broke up when they saw me, and everyone was suddenly busy sticking clothes in lockers and heading for showers. I hadn't really caught on yet. Stupid. Then I saw the book on the bench and I picked it up. At first my stomach felt like it was going to turn inside out, and then I began to burn. But I didn't holler. It came out raspy, like I had a sore throat. "Where'd you get this?" Then I yelled. "Is this what you were reading? My mother's book?"

Sikorski grabbed my arm. "Hey, take it easy. Baxter's just kidding around. Don't get all bent outta shape. It's not as bad as the book he had in here last week."

"Where'd you get it?" I was screaming then.

Eddie Baxter reached over my head and snatched the book right out of my hand. "I know a guy who's reading it in history class, your mother's history class, so bug off."

The coach walked in just then and everyone shut up. "What's going on?" he asked.

"Nothing," Baxter said. "Just kidding around."

Huntley gave us the evil eye. "Better not be any problems. Now get ready." He left.

I pulled off my shirt. Sikorski used the locker next to me. "Hey, the guys were just kidding. Baxter didn't even get to the ripe stuff, you know, where those guys raped the slave women. How does your mother know all that stuff anyway?"

That did it. I swung on him, but I didn't connect because Buzz came up behind and grabbed me in a bear hug. "Easy, Troy. Geez, take it easy, will you?"

I was breathing in big gulps. Sikorski said, "Sorry. I didn't mean anything. Yeah, a writer doesn't have to actually kill someone to write a murder mystery, right?"

"What's that supposed to mean?"

"Nothing." Sikorski shrugged. "Man, I said I'm sorry. Forget it. Come on, let's warm up."

"Yeah, Troy." Buzz gave me a shove toward the door and I followed him out of the locker room, down the wet stairs to the pool.

I cannonballed into the water. It was freezing, but the pain of it made me stop thinking. I did some laps, slow and steady. After a few lengths I hung on the edge of the pool.

Buzz came up snorting like a seal. He shook his head. "What was all the hassle in the locker room? Good way to get kicked off the team, Troy, flying off like that."

I didn't have time to explain. Baxter did a belly flop right over us, and Buzz ducked under to grab his leg. The whistle blew and Coach hollered for us to get out. The officials were talking at one end of the pool and people were finding seats in the bleachers. Eighth grade meets don't get much of a crowd, mostly parents, except when they're the prelim to a varsity meet. We filed back into the locker room and the coach gave us the usual pep talk and all the junk about sportsmanship. He's like a tape recorder. Same every time.

Prescott was an in-between kind of meet, not easy but not impossible. I mean, no pressure really, except that I wanted to win the 100 fly and the last relay. We knew we'd have to hustle for that relay. But Sikorski said he felt fantastic, and Buzz always came through.

Coach read the lineup. It was going to be Sikorski, Chang, the Buzzard, and me as anchor. "All right!" Chang hollered, "we'll do it." We charged out of the locker room and the only thing on my mind then was the meet.

Swim meets are partly like golf and partly like wrestling. I mean, at first when the swimmers are on the block taking their marks, it's so quiet you'd think everyone was watching a champion sink a long putt. But when that gun goes off, the crowd goes crazy. It's like a wrestling match where even the mothers stand up and scream stuff you wouldn't believe. It doesn't matter, though, because you don't even hear it. Not when you concentrate.

The meet moved along. We took the 50 freestyle and they took the 100 free. Baxter cut through the water like a destroyer to take the breaststroke, and Chang got a second in the back. I touched just a fingernail ahead of a Prescott kid for a second in the fly, and Buzz took the first, as usual. Their diver was fantastic. Ours wasn't.

By relay time the score was tied. The other team was hot and they had brought a loud cheering section. Buzz prowled, swinging his arms and loosening up. Chang huddled on the bench like he was in a trance. I walked up and down in front of the bench trying to concentrate, but I kept getting flashes of Baxter reading from Mom's book in the locker room. So I closed my eyes and made myself go through the whole race like a movie playing in my head.

I saw myself on the block, bending low, taking my

mark, hearing the gun. I could almost feel the smack of the water, the shallow dive. Then, all in my head, I pulled a strong, smooth, steady pace, way ahead of the Prescott swimmer.

"Come on, let's go." Buzz touched my shoulder and I followed him to the starting block.

The cheers and screams from the bleachers filled the room and bounced off the tile walls. It was solid noise, no words, just noise. An official held up one hand. The noise died. "Swimmers, take your mark," he called.

Sikorski was on the block, knees bent, arms hanging loose at his sides. "Get set," shouted the started. Sikorski swung his arms back, ready for a strong push off. And then the gun. It's like a shot of adrenaline going straight into your body. It lifts you right off.

Sikorski and the Prescott kid took off together, a matched set. The Prescott guy moved a stroke ahead, but Sikorski made it up on the turn. A perfect flip. The screams washed over us. Sikorski and the other guy touched just milliseconds apart. Chang flew off the block as soon as the official tapped his foot. That's the signal to make sure you don't go too soon. Chang sailed out in a smooth arc, cutting into the water nice and shallow. He surfaced at a good speed. When he pulled a body length ahead of the Prescott guy, the stands went wild.

"Go, man. Go! Go! Go!" we chanted. I could feel the energy build in me with every pull of Chang's arms.

The turn evened them out, and in the home stretch they were practically synchronized swimmers. I couldn't tell who touched the wall first. Buzz pushed off like a loaded spring. I was next. I stepped up on the block, not paying much attention to the Prescott swimmer, but I got the feeling that he kind of swaggered up to his block. I glanced over and saw him adjust his ear plugs.

Buzz had pulled ahead a whole body length, and he was strong. His arms moved like windmills. Man, he's good. I puffed out to empty my lungs and then I took a couple of shallow breaths, then a big deep one that I let out slow. I swung my arms, loosened my legs.

"Take your mark," the official said to me when Buzz was only a stroke away. His hand was next to my foot and I was ready to fly when he tapped me. "Steady," he said.

My eyes were on Buzz, and I had nothing on my mind but the official's signal. Even so, I heard the words coming from the kid on the block next to me.

"Your mother writes dirty books."

I froze. For a split second I froze.

"GO!" shouted my starter. But I'd missed a beat, and the Prescott kid hit the water before me. I went too deep and came up gulping, with one arm caught under the rope that marks the lanes. By the time I got straightened out, I could feel the wake from the Prescott kid's kick.

I pulled. Harder. My lungs were bursting. I hauled water, willing myself to move. The turn was okay. I flipped and got a good push. But the Prescott kid was ahead. I tried. God, I tried. On the home stretch I trailed a body length behind. I made up some of it, but not enough. Not enough. My arms were lead weights. I grabbed the end of the pool and laid my head in the gutter. I wanted to die.

Someone leaned down and offered a hand to help me

out. I didn't take it. We lost. My fault. All my fault.

I pulled myself out of the pool. "Too bad, son. Rough start." The official patted my shoulder, but I shoved by him. He slipped and fell backward, splat on the wet tile. I didn't even look back. I pushed Buzz away, Sikorski and Chang, too. I grabbed my towel off the bench, covered my face, and started for the locker room. The Prescott crowd was going nuts, screaming and cheering like they'd won the Olympics.

The coach grabbed my arm with a grip that would snap a bone. "What's the matter with you?" he growled. "Unsportsmanlike conduct. You're out!" He mumbled something about discipline and training and all that junk.

"I quit!" I screamed just before the locker room door swung shut behind me.

7

The locker room was packed with the whole varsity team getting undressed. "Hey, squirt, how'd you make out? Did you win?" someone yelled.

I pushed past two huge guys and grabbed my clothes out of my locker. Out in the hall, I hopped on one leg while I pulled my jeans on over my wet trunks. Real graceful athlete.

It felt good to be outside, but the sidewalk was freezing on my bare feet so I sat on the curb and crammed my sneakers on. And then I walked.

I kicked a stone and sent it sailing across the street. Why had I flown off like that? A dumb, stupid jerk, that's what I was. Act now, think later — real smart, Troy. So what should I do? Go home and get yelled at? Or just keep walking? I decided to walk for a while first. I knew I'd have to explain to Mom eventually, and she'd make me apologize to the coach even if it was thirty-seven years from now. I hoped that official was okay. I hadn't meant to knock him down, for Pete's sake. Why didn't the coach know that?

Usually there's nothing I liked better than walking

alone on a spring night when the leaves are just starting to pop, and the streetlights make wet sidewalks look slick and shiny. I like the smell of wet lawns, and the way everything seems so clean and sweet. And I like to look into lighted houses and see people watching TV or reading newspapers while I'm free outside. But not tonight. Tonight I felt left out.

A car cruised through a puddle next to the curb and splashed me, but I didn't even care. Maybe it was my night to be dumped on. I shivered as I turned down Maple Street and headed for home.

Every light in the house was on — it looked like a commercial for the electric company. And they were waiting.

Mom first. "Where have you been?"

Then Gram. "Are you all right?"

Mom again. "The coach called three times."

My swim trunks felt like a sticky octopus had grabbed me, and I was hungry and I just wanted to be left alone. I exploded at Mom. "You taking attendance? You're not in any damn class now. Can't a guy go anywhere without checking in every second?"

"That's enough!" Mom glared at me.

Gram touched Mom's shoulder. "Now, Martha, take it easy."

But Mom pulled away. "Don't interfere." Gram looked as if Mom had slapped her, but she stuck her chin in the air and marched into the kitchen as though she had meant to leave anyway.

It was like the shoot-out at the old corral. The two gunfighters face to face at high noon. Mom went first.

"What happened? What on earth made you knock down an official and stomp off like that?"

"I didn't knock him down. He slipped."

Mom was sizzling, but she waited.

"So I'm sorry. Okay? I was mad at myself for losing the relay, that's all. The guy slipped."

"Oh come now, you've lost before. Obviously it was more than that. What happened?"

"Nothing. I'm telling you, nothing!" I grabbed my swim bag and headed for the stairs. What could I tell her, that we lost the meet because of her dumb book? That I couldn't handle it?

"Luther, come back here." It was an order. I stopped on the third step.

"Tomorrow morning you'll apologize to the coach, is that clear?"

"Oh, yeah, that's clear. Everything's really clear." I stomped upstairs and slammed my bedroom door so hard that Jez scrambled off my bed like she'd been shot.

Saturday morning the trumpets woke me up. I buried my head under the pillow. The one Saturday without early swim practice and Maggie turns on cartoons at dawn. The trumpets got louder. Then the drums, a slow, loud beat. For a second I thought I'd left the stereo on, but the beat got louder.

I rolled out of bed. "Shut off the TV or turn it down," I hollered. I collided with Maggie in the hall.

"It's not me." She stuck out her tongue.

Gram was right behind her. "What on earth is that?"

She blinked and tied her red bathrobe tighter. "Wait, I need my glasses."

By this time the noise was thumping through the house full blast. Mom stumbled out of her room. "What's going on?" She looked half asleep. We all shuffled downstairs like zombies. I hadn't even stopped to put on my bathrobe, and Maggie was in her pajamas, too. Jez galloped around us as though she thought it was high time we woke up.

Even half asleep I figured out the noise was coming from our front yard. When I opened the door Jez raced out, barking and yipping. "Jez, get back here," I yelled, but that just sent her into circles, chasing her tail.

Maggie squeezed by me. "A parade. They're having a parade." She danced to the end of the porch. It was a parade all right, with flags flying, trumpets blaring, and kids following on bikes.

"What's going on?" Mom asked.

Gram shivered. "I don't like this, Martha."

"This is fun, this is fun," Maggie chanted.

But I didn't like it either. "Shut up, Maggot."

There was one loud whap of the biggest drum out front and the guy carrying it shouted, "Company halt."

They did. It was like all the sound in the world had been turned off for a second. Mom smoothed her hair and tied her bathrobe tighter. "What's going on here?"

The guy in front gave his drum one more thump. "We've come on a mission of concern from all the good people of this community."

"Yeah, the good people," someone echoed. A big lady waved a sign that said "Clean Books, Clean Minds" in sparkling letters above a huge picture of Major Madison.

Two kids carried a long skinny banner between them that said "The Marching Moralists," like it was some kind of drum and bugle corps.

There must have been about fifty people in the crowd and they were all wearing white straw hats . . . well, plastic that looked like straw . . . with red, white, and blue ribbons. At first they all looked alike, but then I saw a couple of people I knew. The barber. What was he doing here? And a lady who worked at the bank. She was carrying a sign that said "Crusade for Clean Minds."

Eddie Baxter's mother was handing out pamphlets. Eddie was slinking along behind her, kind of scrunched down like he wanted to hide.

"What do you want? Why are you here?" Mom called.

"We're here on behalf of the Crusade for a Clean America. We represent Major Madison," said the man in front. He said it like he was talking about God himself.

Mom took a step forward. "Please get off our lawn and leave us alone. You're disturbing our peace."

The guy next door opened his window and hollered, "What the heck's going on? It's Saturday, you idiots. Can the noise. This used to be a decent neighborhood."

Doors and windows all up and down the street opened. Mrs. Kramer across the street was still in her bathrobe, too, but she was sweeping her porch so fast she could have taken off on her broom. A couple of cars slowed down and kids on bikes did wheelies on our lawn. I shouted at them, "Get off the grass."

Mrs. Baxter took four strides closer to our porch. "This

is an informational march." She looked around as though she wanted everyone to agree with her. "We mean you no harm, Martha. This is just our way of attracting attention and inviting everyone to clean their homes of books and records and videos that clutter the minds of our youth with evil ideas."

Some of the marchers shouted, "Yeah," and "Hooray for a clean America." Two men handed pamphlets to neighbors who had wandered over to watch the show.

Mom leaned against the porch railing. "Why did you come here? We're not part of your campaign." I couldn't believe it when she added, "And what does it have to do with us?"

This time a lady stepped out from the middle of the bunch. She waved a little American flag a couple of times, then she cleared her throat. I thought she'd shout like the rest of them, but she had a chirpy voice that made me think of starlings. "Oh come now, Mrs. Troy. Surely you realize how you've contributed to this, this, uh, well surely you must understand your role in this. And you can help, truly you can."

When Mom didn't answer, the lady kept on. "Your book, don't you know. The romance, that passion thing. It's in the school now, and we can't have that, can we?" She waved her little flag like a nervous squirrel shaking its tail. "If you will withdraw your book from the history class, it will save quite a lot of fuss."

"What do you mean, fuss?" Mom asked her.

The drum-banger yelled, "She means it will save you the embarrassment of having a petition presented to the school board, that's what fuss. We don't intend our young people to be exposed to dirty books, no ma'am." He whapped his drum.

Mom's face was white and Gram's was getting red. She was peering out at the crowd when suddenly she gasped. "Arthur Hastings! You should be ashamed of yourself." She glared at him. "Don't you ever call on me again."

Mr. Hastings pulled his hat down low over his eyes, and he sidled over to stand behind a taller man.

A few people laughed. But Mom had reached her boiling point. "Get out of here before I call the police," she said. She turned then and pushed Gram and me toward the door. In her hurry to get us all into the house, she almost tripped over Maggie. Jez stayed on the porch, barking her heart out with no one telling her to shut up.

After a few minutes we heard the band march on down the street, drums banging, horns tooting.

Mom stormed into the kitchen and started opening cupboard doors. She slammed the frying pan on the stove so hard the lid flew off and clanged across the floor. Gram elbowed Mom out of the way. "Out, out," she told Mom gently. "Go on upstairs and get dressed. I'll handle breakfast."

Mom fussed and fumed, muttering to herself and wiping her eyes, but finally she went upstairs. Gram said, "Come on Luke. Give me a hand." She called Maggie. "Get dressed, sweetie, and then you can mix the pancakes for me." When Maggie was out of the kitchen, Gram said, "Oh, Luke, what are we going to do? Your poor mother."

"Poor mother? Oh yeah, that's great — poor mother!

Nuts. She's the one who started all this with that stupid book." I grabbed a banana and started to rip the skin off.

Gram's eyes bored into me, but I ignored the signal. "You got any idea how the guys are hassling me?" I said. "I mean, there I am on the starting block last night and this kid next to me says my mother writes dirty books."

Gram's eyebrows flew up. "Yeah, how do you think that made me feel?" I said. "If Mom has to write that kind of stuff, why can't she keep it quiet. Why the heck did she have to tell her class to read the book? Man, she talks about me seeing only my side. What about her?"

That did it. Gram attacked. "Luther Alexander Troy, if I weren't your grandmother I'd smack you. Have you any idea what you're talking about? Did you read her book? Do you know what it's about?"

"Yeah, well, I read some parts."

"Parts? You only read parts of your own mother's book?"

I was burying myself. No matter how I tried to explain it, Gram wasn't going to understand. "Well, you know, I like science fiction, and gee, Gram, romance is. . . ." I trailed off because she looked ready to explode.

Maggie skipped into the kitchen and saved me. Gram swallowed whatever she was going to say, and Maggie pushed the stool over to the table. "I'm ready, Grammy. I even washed my hands. You said I could mix the pancakes."

Maggie giggled when I headed for the back door, and Gram even waited until I pulled it open before she stopped me with, "Luke, you're still wearing your pajamas."

8

When I finally got myself together, I cruised around on my bike for a while, then headed for Buzz's house. He lives not far from us, but in those few blocks, I followed the tracks of the Crusade parade. A couple of ripped banners and pamphlets blew across lawns, and before I turned the corner at Buzz's street, I rode right over the Major's face smiling up from a torn poster.

I spun around in a spectacular wheelie so I could run over that face again. I wished I'd never seen it, never heard of Major Madison or his dumb crusade. If only I'd been listening in English class that day when Mrs. Lester assigned interviews, maybe I wouldn't have gone along with Buzz when he chose the Major, and Mom's book would never have come into the discussion. Well, too late now. I jerked my bike into a sharp turn once more, and this time I jammed the brakes to a fast stop that shredded the Major's face under my tire.

At Buzz's house, I pounded on the back door because their doorbell's broken, but there was no answer so I shoved it open. "Hey, anybody home?"

"In here," Buzz hollered.

"In here" was the dining room. I couldn't believe it. Buzz was on his hands and knees slapping paste on a strip of wallpaper. His mother was on a ladder, reaching up to smooth down a hunk of blue flowered paper; but just as I walked in, a huge flap peeled off in slow motion and plopped on her head.

"Help," Mrs. Ryan yelled but it was muffled under the thick paper. She bent over and struggled to slide the wallpaper off. I grabbed one end of the paper but it peeled away in a strip like a soggy noodle and came all the way off the wall. That broke up Buzz into one of his snorting laughs that makes him sound like a bull with asthma.

Mrs. Ryan wiped a path through the gooey paste on her face and blinked. Her eyelashes stuck and she wiped at them again. "Get out of here!" She laughed, too, and looked at Buzz. "You're about as much help as your father. We almost got a divorce over wallpapering together!"

"Sorry, Ma. You can't get rid of me that easy. No child divorce laws in this state."

"Children! Who needs them?" Mrs. Ryan shook her head, but she hugged Buzz and gave him a smack on the cheek, smearing him with paste, too.

"Yuck! Thanks a million. Now I'm really stuck with you."

His mother headed for the bathroom, but she called, "If you and Luke go out, be sure you're home by noon. Dad's got some plans."

Buzz washed up at the kitchen sink. "Good timing," he said. "Anything to get out of wallpapering. So what's up?

What the heck happened to you last night? I called you a couple of times but your mom said you weren't home. Where'd you go? The coach had us searching the school for you."

I shrugged. "What can I say? I blew it."

"I'll say." Buzz grabbed two glazed doughnuts from the table and handed me one. "But why'd you run off? Geez, we've lost before and it never threw you like that."

When I didn't explain, Buzz knew enough to let it go. He shrugged and asked, "So what's up? What're you going to do now?"

"Nothing. I just had to get out. Want to ride to the mall?"

"Okay. Why not?"

We were on the way out when Buzz's mom stuck her head in the kitchen doorway. "Any chance you'd like to come for dinner tonight, Luke?"

Buzz had a mouthful of doughnut but he choked it down. "Yeah. Terrific. Stay overnight, too. We'll watch a video and just junk around."

I stood there nodding my head like one of those bobbing birds on a car dashboard before I remembered why I couldn't. "Nuts, I can't," I said. "I promised Mom I'd stay with Maggie tonight."

"Oh, I'm sorry," Buzz's mom said. "Your mother is so lucky to have a built-in babysitter."

"Yeah, real lucky," I mumbled.

"So come over tomorrow instead," Buzz said. "I'll ask Dad to take us to the Go-Kart track after church. Okay, Mom?"

After his mom agreed that would be all right, Buzz got his bike out of the garage and we headed toward the mall. Buzz rode ahead of me, so we didn't talk, but when we stopped for a red light, I pulled up next to him. "Did you see the parade?"

"What parade? When?"

"The Major's Crusade thing. Didn't you hear it this morning? They made enough noise to move rocks. Stomped all over our lawn, too," I said.

"Yeah, I thought I heard a band playing, but I figured it was someone's stereo on loud," Buzz said. "They didn't come down our street. So what were they parading for?"

"Aw gee, they're trying to hassle my mom." Just thinking about it made me mad again and I pulled away, pumping so hard my lungs felt like they were full of molten lead.

"Hey, wait up," Buzz hollered.

By the time he caught up to me I'd cooled off enough to ask him, "Did you read my mom's book?"

"Are you kidding? Me? Nah, I stick to sports stuff. Did you? Read her book, I mean."

"Yeah, sort of," I admitted.

"What do you mean, sort of? You mean the hot parts Sikorski marked? Yeah, everyone read those."

Buzz knew I'd read them too, and it made me feel creepy. This dumb book was really bugging me. Why should I read it? I hate mushy stuff. What'd my mother expect? I was glad she got the book published, but why did she have to take it to school? I couldn't see why she didn't just call up the Major or someone on that Crusade committee and tell them she wouldn't let her students read it anymore. Then the whole thing would be over. It didn't have to be such a big deal.

Buzz rode along next to me for a while and finally he said, "Want to see if the new *Road and Track* is in?"

"Sure." At the mall we stuck our bikes in the beat-up hunk of metal they call a bike rack, and locked them.

"Got any cash?" Buzz asked.

I dug through my pockets. "About seventy-nine cents, maybe eighty. Wait a sec." I remembered a dollar in one of the little zippered pockets of my jacket. "Not exactly rich, but I can go halves on the magazine."

"Big spender Troy. Naw, don't worry. Mom paid me to help her this morning. I've got bucks."

"Some help," I said. Buzz knew I was kidding so he ignored me. We ambled past a couple of shoe stores and the vitamin booth and the ear-piercing booth. Right in front of Waldenbooks we ran into Eddie Baxter. That was all I needed. I grabbed Buzz. "Come on, let's go."

But Buzz jerked his arm away and called to Eddie, "Hey, Baxter, what's up? Want to hang out with us?"

"Can't," Baxter said. "My mom signed me up to help with her booth."

"Yeah? What's she selling?" Buzz wanted to know.

"Nothing. She's, well geez Troy, I'm sorry. She's making me hand out these stupid pamphlets."

I grabbed one from Eddie. It said, "Clean books for clean minds." I ripped it in half and threw it at him.

"Eddie? I need you." It was Mrs. Baxter. She was standing behind a table draped in red, white, and blue cloth. A bunch of other people were there, too, and all of them wore those dumb plastic hats with the flags like the paraders wore. I don't think I even said anything to Buzz. I just knew I had to get out of there fast.

I almost tripped over a kid's stroller as I plowed my way through shoppers, and I didn't answer when Buzz yelled for me to wait. I got my bike from the rack and headed out of town. For a while I rode past some farms. Two huge black dogs came roaring out from behind a barn and scared the heck out of me, but otherwise I just rolled along. It was nice to be alone. I wondered what my dad was doing. Would it've been different if he'd stayed with us? I hadn't seen him since I was a little kid, but sometimes when I felt all hollow like this, I would have liked to have had a father around. But hey, maybe he was a creep or a loser, or why would he have left us? I tried to think about something else. Finally I headed back to town, stopped at McDonald's, and spent my $1.79.

Back home, Mom was on the phone, Gram was out, and Maggie was playing dress-up with some kids on the porch. Jez followed me up to my room. Everything looked neat. But not neat enough! I tore the blankets and sheets off the bed and knocked all the books and models off the shelves. I grabbed stuff from the closet and dragged it out and piled it in the middle of the room. When it looked like a garbage dump, I felt better, like I wasn't going to explode and splatter everything with blood and guts.

I spent the rest of the afternoon going through my stuff and getting it all organized again.

Buzz called. "What happened? What's the matter with

you? Why'd you take off like that? I thought you wanted to hang out at the mall. You're getting weird, Troy."

"Sorry. I just, aw, no reason." How could I explain? I couldn't even sort out my own feelings. "Is it still on for the Go-Kart track tomorrow?"

Buzz said it was and told me when his dad would pick me up. "It'll be great," he promised.

Dinner that night was bad. I don't mean the food, I mean the way Mom and Gram and I were super-polite and only said stuff like, "Please pass the macaroni and cheese."

After that it settled into a regular kind of Saturday night. Mom went to the movies with a couple of friends, Gram went roller skating without Art, and I babysat. After three games of Go Fish, and two of Chutes and Ladders, I'd had enough. "Want to watch TV, kid?" I finally asked Maggie.

"Did Mommy say it was all right?" Maggie wasn't going to take my word for anything.

"Sure. I'll make popcorn." That was okay with the Maggot, and we both fell asleep on the couch with the TV still blasting.

*

Sunday morning I was ready an hour before Buzz and his dad picked me up. Buzz's dad doesn't look anything like the car salesmen you see in television ads. He's real quiet and kind of gentle. You can tell he likes you by the way he listens to anything you say. "So how's it going, Luke?" he asked as soon as I got in the car.

"Okay, Mr. Ryan. Just fine."

He nodded like he believed me, and then we talked about swim meets until we got to the track. I was surprised when Mr. Ryan asked the man at the gate for three carts. Buzz said, "Wait till you see him. Dad thinks he's Paul Newman when he gets on a track."

Mr. Ryan laughed. "I'm better." He folded his long legs into one of the small carts. "Let's go. I'll treat the losers after the race."

And he did. He took us to Harvey's Happy Ice Cream Store where they make hot fudge sundaes worth dying for. We had just dug into ours when two men and a woman walked into the restaurant. They were wearing white plastic hats and big round buttons showing the Major's smiling face.

"Hey, aren't those some of the people we saw at the mall with Eddie's mother?" Buzz asked me.

I had a mouthful of ice cream so I didn't answer, but Mr. Ryan turned around just as one of the men approached our table. He handed Buzz's dad a pamphlet. "You'll be interested in this," he said, "especially with two such fine-looking boys as yours. We hope you'll read our message and join our Crusade."

I held my breath as Mr. Ryan took the pamphlet, frowned, and then handed it back. "No, thank you," he said louder than he usually talks. "My wife and I prefer to rely on good sense rather than censorship." He smiled at us. "Finish your sundaes, boys, and let's get out of here."

The Crusade guy glared at us. "So you're one of those," he said to Mr. Ryan. "Well, I hope you know what you're doing to fine young minds."

Mr. Ryan took his time wiping his mouth and folding his paper napkin before he said, "I'm not sure I know what you mean by 'one of those,' but I do indeed know enough to encourage fine young minds. Good-bye." Then he said to us, "Come on, boys, let's go."

All the way home, Mr. Ryan told stories and jokes. I'd never seen him act like that, as though he were trying to cheer me up and make me forget about those Crusaders. When we got to my house, he couldn't even pull into the driveway because there were so many cars around. "Is your mother having a party?" Mr. Ryan asked.

"Not that I know about. Guess I'll go in the back way. I had a great time. Thanks a lot, Mr. Ryan. See you, Buzz."

Before I closed the car door, Mr. Ryan leaned over and said, "We had a good time, too, Luke. It's always nice to have you around." Then he gave me a thumbs-up sign. "Chin up. Lots of people are on your mother's team."

I could here the laughing and shrieking before I opened the back door. Women were everywhere. Even Jez didn't pay much attention to me; she was too busy licking up crumbs under the kitchen table. A lady was pulling a pan of good-smelling stuff out of the oven. She said, "Hello, you must be Luther. You're just in time for my hot crab rolls. Grab a plate."

"Sure, okay. Thanks." I stuck a crab roll in my mouth, but it was so hot it made my eyes water. I almost bumped into Mom, who was carrying a tray of empty glasses to the kitchen.

"Hi honey. Did you have fun? Are you hungry?"

I fanned my mouth and nodded a yes. Then I gulped

the crab roll fast. "Terrific time. What's going on?"

"It's my writing group and the Friends of the Library. We're making posters for the rally."

Two ladies were on their knees in the dining room. One was painting letters on a sign. "I can't fit the word censorship on here. Give me a shorter slogan."

The other lady laughed, only it was more of a cackle. "Put the words in a circle."

Another woman was folding papers at the dining room table and stacking them into a box. I could see Gram, biting her lower lip while she slammed a staple gun, fastening signs to sticks. Even Maggie was working. She followed Gram around picking up the staples that flew on the floor and holding the squares of cardboard on the sticks for Gram.

The living room was packed, too. Sikorski's mother was squeezed between two other women on the couch. She waved and yelled, "Hi, Luther." I'd seen a lot of the people when Mom's writing group met at our house, but I didn't remember their names. Mom came up behind me and put her arm around my shoulder. "This is my son, Luke," she called over the noise. "He'll help us distribute the signs at the rally Friday."

For a split second I thought of Eddie, and I wondered if his mother had made the same announcement. The noise level went through the roof as everyone shrilled their version of hello and oh-how-nice.

I vaulted the first three steps in one spectacular leap and made it to the safety of my room faster than any human. If they ever have an Olympic event for escape, I'm in for the gold.

9

"**D**id you apologize to Coach Huntley?" Mom tossed that at me first thing Monday morning. I gulped my orange juice before I told her I hadn't. "This morning, young man. Please talk to him this morning. If you're ready I'll drop you off at school."

I grabbed a banana, my lunch, and my books. "Yeah, I'm ready." In the car I was tying my sneakers when Mom hit me with the big one.

"Luther, I've been meaning to ask you. What did you think of *The Passionate Pirate*? You did read it, didn't you?"

Fortunately my mouth was full of banana and my "not yet" came out more like "nofflet." She let it drop, but the subject was open now and I knew I'd have to read the thing.

Suddenly Mom shouted, "Hey, you lowlife!" She swung the wheel hard and the car swerved just in time to miss a blue van that didn't bother to stop at a sign. She muttered some other stuff under her breath, and by the time she cooled off we were in front of the school. "Oh no," Mom moaned. "Don't tell me they're going to picket the school. This is too much."

About fifteen people were walking in a circle around the flagpole. They all wore the white plastic-straw hats I hated by now. Most of them carried signs that said "Rid Our Schools of Smut."

Mom pulled into the parking lot. As I started to get out of the car, she put a hand on my arm. She looked worn-out and the day had only started. "It's going to be all right," she said. "We'll talk about it later. And you'll see the coach, won't you? You'll apologize?"

"Sure, Mom."

"Have a good day, honey."

"Yeah, you too, Mom. Don't let them get you down."

I could hardly keep my eyes open in English class because my desk is next to the window and the sun bakes me. I could see the marchers, going around and around and around. It was easy to count the number of times they circled the flagpole if I started each round with Mrs. Baxter because she towered over the others. But even counting, I had to blink to keep my eyes open.

None of the other kids near the window were paying any attention to Mrs. Lester either because of the action around the flagpole. Then, when a television crew showed up, even Mrs. Lester bustled to the window. "Maybe this is a more important lesson," she told us as she watched the marchers. "Yes, I think we need to talk about censorship." She turned to face us again. "I'd like to hear your opinions."

"Hey, nobody's censoring anything. They just want to get the cruddy stuff outta school." We all swiveled around to see who had dropped that one. It was Eddie. He was slumped so far down in his seat that his legs stuck out in the aisle like oars in a boat.

"You creep." I was already half out of my seat but Mrs. Lester's strong right arm pushed me down. Everyone went nuts, all talking at once.

Mrs. Lester whapped her ruler on the desk. "All right. Enough! One at a time," she ordered. "We'll do this in a civilized manner or not at all. First we'll have to decide what censorship is. And then we should talk about censors. Who can tell you what you may or may not read? Who chooses your books?"

"Hey, nobody tells me what to read." I didn't know who said that, but it came from the back of the room.

"Are you sure of that?" Mrs. Lester asked us. "Who buys the books for the library? Someone chooses those. And who buys the books at your house? Who chooses the books to be sold in bookstores? Doesn't Mr. Krupnik at the drugstore choose what magazines he'll sell?" That took a few seconds to sink in.

Old Lester knew when to press her point. "And how about editors and publishers? Certainly they choose what should be in print in the first place, do they not? Does everything that's written get into print?"

"Hey, maybe not," Sikorski said. "But nobody tells you what you can read, from the stuff that gets printed, I mean."

"Right," someone shouted.

"Is the right to read part of our guarantee of free speech?" Mrs. Lester was asking more questions than she was answering. Then she got to the main one. "And what about choosing books to use in classrooms? Do teachers have the right to select books for their courses? How do you feel about the fact that those people picketing out there want Mrs. Troy's book banned from her history class?"

For once the bell rang too soon, and at first nobody moved. But in that second Mrs. Lester really nailed me. "Perhaps the best way to learn about Mrs. Troy's book is from Luther. Will you do that, Luke? Will you be prepared tomorrow to summarize *The Passionate Pirate*?"

She might as well have punched me in the head. I didn't hear anything after that. It was like I was under a glass dome as I walked down the hall. I could see mouths moving, but nothing came through. Buzz was talking to me, but it didn't sink in. I was wondering if I should go back and tell Mrs. Lester to ask my mom to talk to the class instead of me. Yeah, that would do it. She'd think that was great and Mom wouldn't mind. Maybe she'd even like to have the chance.

I circled back to Mrs. Lester's room. "Hey, Troy, where're you going?" Buzz called.

"Got something to do. See you later." I got to Mrs. Lester's room just as she was locking the door. But she listened when I explained that having my mother would be better than me talking about her book.

Mrs. Lester jangled her keys impatiently. "Hmm. Yes, you're right. I do want your mother to talk to the class about writing, but I'd really like to get your view of this, Luther. Yes, I'd like you to review the book." She turned and stalked away.

I slogged through the rest of the day at school, just sort of went through the motions. Mostly I wondered how the heck I was going to get that book read by tomorrow. It was more than three hundred pages long, and I had a ton of math homework, too. Maybe if I got Gram talking about the story, I'd find out enough to fake it. I even went home right after school, but Gram was out shopping so I didn't get a chance to talk to her.

After supper, Mom was correcting papers at one end of the dining room table, and Gram was at the other end helping Maggie with her spelling words. When I came down from my room for a refill of Pepsi, Mom heard me in the kitchen. "Luke. What did the coach say?"

Oh nuts, the coach. I'd forgotten all about that. "Nothing, Mom. I didn't talk to him."

That made her put down her red pencil. "Why not?"

"He wasn't there." The lie came easy. It just slipped out.

I thought she was looking right through me. "Okay. But tomorrow for sure. I mean it, Luke. You can't put it off."

"Okay, okay." Then I figured this might be as good a time as any. "Listen, Mom. Can you do me a favor?"

"Maybe. Depends." She was whipping her red pencil down some kid's paper, checking off true and false.

"Mrs. Lester asked me to review your book, you know kind of tell about it in class tomorrow."

The red pencil stopped. "Ah, and let me guess. You want a quick condensed version, right?"

"Yeah, that'd be great."

"I'm sure it would." The red pencil was tapping the

table now. Gram put down the notebook and Maggie stopped right in the middle of spelling "wonder." "Well, forget it, my dear. You haven't read the book, have you?"

"Hey, sure I have." The pencil was going double time. "Well, parts of it," I admitted.

"Parts?"

"Gee Mom, I've been busy, you know. I mean with swim practice and watching Maggie and everything. . . ."

"Parts!" She said it again. "Ah, yes, the famous under-lined pages." Boy, she didn't need to sound so snotty.

I shrugged. "Yeah, well what'd you expect? The guys had it in the locker room, and sure I read it."

Mom didn't say anything for a second. She put down the red pencil, and sighed. "You really think I wrote a dirty book, don't you?"

I took a gulp of Pepsi so I wouldn't have to answer.

"Look at me! Answer me!"

"Hey, I'm not just another kid at school, Mom. It's your business, and I don't care. Just leave me out of it, okay?"

For a second I thought she was going to get up and hit me, but she never had except for once when I was four and ran into the street without looking. Instead she clenched her jaw so hard it looked like it was carved in rock. Gram started to say something, but Mom put her hand out to stop her.

"You're right, Luke," Mom said. "It is my business. Apparently you can't see that it's also yours."

"Okay, okay. I'll read it. Where's the book? I'll read it right now."

Mom's eyes flashed, her danger signal. "Don't do me

any favors." She started to say something else but Gram moved in.

"Stop this, both of you. Martha, leave the boy alone. And Luther, stop acting like a spoiled brat." Gram got up and rummaged through a pile of papers on the window seat. "Here. Here's the book. Go on upstairs and read it, Luke. Go on, now."

I grabbed the book. I was on my way upstairs when I heard Maggie say, "What's everybody so mad about? Who got Mommy's book dirty?"

10

The Passionate Pirate by Antonia Tyson. I stared at the cover. Buzz was right. It sure looked like a dirty book. The lady's dress was cut so low it didn't leave you guessing about much. I flipped to the dedication page. Mom had shown me that when the book came from the publisher and we had a big celebration. I read it again.

Dedicated to my children, Luke and Margaret, and my mother Ruth, who believed in me and helped so much.

I wasn't sure what she meant by us believing in her; that part must have been mostly for Gram because half the time I didn't even know what Mom was writing. In that TV interview Mom had said how much we helped, too, and I wondered if people would think she meant we helped her write the book. I guess not, but I'll bet they didn't know she meant babysitting and stuff like that.

On the next page I read a couple of lines I hadn't noticed before.

*

In praise of men and women everywhere, in every generation, who fight passionately for their beliefs.

I put the stereo on low, punched up the pillows, and made sure I could reach the Pepsi and a bag of chips. I was ready to read.

Chapter One

The ship heaved on each wave, and rolled down into the next deep trough. Matthew Hull's stomach rolled and heaved with it. When he thought he had nothing left inside him, he threw up again, too weak to move from his narrow bunk.

For a while he lay there, praying to be home again, to be dead, whichever was possible first. Home. The thought of it made him move, and he hauled himself to his feet, forcing himself to drag one foot after the other to the ladder. No one noticed the young cabin boy. The men sprawled in the other cramped, filthy bunks were too miserable to do more than keep themselves alive.

Fresh air. I have to get some air, Matt thought. The stench from the cargo bay filled his lungs like a sickening fog. He pulled himself to the top of the ladder and pushed at the closed hatch overhead. It didn't budge. For a minute he hung there, gasping, waiting for strength to try again.

With a mighty heave he tried once more, and

this time the hatch cover moved. The rush of night air hit him like a blow. He breathed deeply of the cold, salty air. As he pulled himself to his feet, an enormous wave of freezing water cascaded across the deck and smashed him against a coil of rope.

The ship dropped into another trough, another wave pounded Matt's slim body. But this time when the ship heaved, and the wave sluiced back into the sea, Matt grabbed the rope. He had no thought of time. It could have been an hour or a lifetime he lay there until, at last, the ocean became a gentle cradle.

Stars appeared once more over the endless sea, and the moans and cries from the dark hold echoed like tortured ghosts in the night. Matt shivered. His wet clothes clung to him. He clenched his teeth to keep them from chattering. At least he was cleansed of the vomit. But the smell of evil from below pervaded the ship and Matthew knew it would stay with him forever.

From the day he had been captured and carried aboard the slave ship and pressed into service as a cabin boy, Matthew had lived for one thing. Escape. He knew he would escape, but now he was driven by another goal . . . revenge. Revenge for himself, for being torn from his mother and father, and revenge for the miserable black bodies stacked like cargo in the ship's stinking hold.

*

I didn't realize how long I'd been reading until I stopped for another refill of Pepsi. Gram is always saying, "Where did the time go?" and now I knew what she meant. I'd been reading for a couple of hours, but it seemed like minutes. This wasn't just some dumb romance.

I punched up the pillows again, opened another can of Pepsi, and picked up the book. I had come to a really awful scene before the slave ship gets to America when Matthew sees some of the sailors rape the black women, young girls really. I'd skimmed through a couple of pages of the scene that time the guys had the book in the locker room, but I hadn't known how it fit into the whole story. Now I could see that scene was the turning point in Matthew Hull's life. It's what made him so mad that he wanted revenge.

But it wasn't sexy or hot. The rapes, I mean. If you read just a few sentences here and there, it might seem to be. But not the whole thing. It made you gag, but it sure didn't turn you on. Talk about violence. This wasn't mushy romance, not when guys are hurting women like that. I knew then that if Mom had just told about the rape, you wouldn't know how disgusting it really was. She had to show it so you'd feel like you were there. I was beginning to understand why Mom wanted her high school seniors to read her story.

I kept reading, and the last thing I remember was that I'd gotten to the part where Matthew Hull was grown up, and he was on a ship, but this time it was his own ship and he was a pirate. Only the amazing thing was that he was a good guy, see. He was trying to capture slave ships and rescue the slaves to get them back to Africa.

The next thing I knew, someone was shaking me. For a second I didn't know where I was. "Luke, wake up. You'll be late for school."

I sat up and the book slipped off the bed. Gram turned off the stereo. "You fell asleep with your light and stereo on. Must have been a good book." She smiled. "Come on, dear. Breakfast's waiting."

I moaned. "Aw, Gram." But I was talking to myself. I blinked and scratched and stared at the guppies. I felt like I was in a trance, but I shuffled into the john.

Mom called from the bottom of the stairs. "Luke, are you ready? Want to ride with me?"

I staggered to the top of the stairs. "I'm sick."

That brought Mom up to my room fast. She put her hand on my forehead. "You don't feel hot. But you do look pale."

"I feel awful." I was only partly faking. I didn't know how late it was before I fell asleep the night before, but now I felt like I could sleep for a month.

I could almost see the battle in Mom's head between mother and teacher, but finally she said, "Well, all right. But you stay in bed."

Gram was hovering around. "Don't worry. I'll take care of him."

I didn't like the way she said that. When I was little she used to give me yucky cough medicine when I was sick. But now she just tucked the covers around me and patted my head. "Sleep. We'll talk later."

I woke up starving, and my legs were numb, but that was only because Jez was sleeping on them. I shoved her off and hollered, "Gram." No answer, so I went downstairs. A note was propped against a box of cereal on the kitchen table. "I went to the grocery store. Be right back. Love, Gram." I wondered how long "right back" would be, but as long as there was food around it didn't matter too much. After I ate a bowl of cereal and bananas and drank a glass of orange juice, I realized it was noon, so I made a peanut butter sandwich and went back to bed. I was on the last chapter of Mom's book when Gram called, "I'm home."

When I got downstairs, Gram was in the kitchen yanking things out of grocery bags and slamming them on the counter and muttering, "I don't believe some people."
"What's the matter, Gram?"
"Hi, dear. You look better. You feel better?"
"Yeah. I feel great."
"Hungry?"
"Just a little. What's up?"
"Luther, I think the world is full of crazy people." She slammed a cupboard shut. "I waited patiently at that checkout counter until I couldn't stand it one more minute. Two perfectly intelligent women."
"Who, Gram? What are you talking about?"
"I'm talking about two women ahead of me in line. Not only did they take forever with their coupons, but they were talking about the rally. They're going to clean out their bookshelves, for heaven's sake, as though it's some kind of flea market." Gram was really steaming. "I don't think they've given the censorship issue a single thought."
I folded the empty grocery bags as Gram emptied them.

"I read Mom's book and I'm almost done. Just a couple more pages."

Gram sat down. "And what do you think?"

"Boy, it's something. How'd Mom come up with the idea? How'd she find out about all that slavery stuff?"

"Why don't you ask her? I think she'd like to know your reaction to the book." Gram got up to put the teakettle on the stove. "It hasn't been easy for her, Luke, not writing the book and certainly not this awful Crusade."

"Then why'd she do it? I mean if she knew it was going to get people all riled up, why didn't she write a different story?"

Gram shook her head. "Oh, Luther. For lots of reasons. She believes in truth, for one." Then Gram grinned.

"Yeah, I know what you're thinking. But I wasn't faking totally. I mean I was telling the truth. I really didn't feel good this morning."

The phone rang and Gram answered it. "Yes, dear. He's all right. Yes, I'm sure we'll manage." She turned away from me, but not before I saw her worried frown. "Oh no! I'm sorry, but I'm sure things will work out. You'll see. Keep your chin up, dear." She hung up. "That was your mother."

I'd guessed that. "What's wrong?"

"Wrong? Why nothing. Your mother has to go to a dinner meeting. She'll be home late."

"Come on, Gram. I'm not a two year old. You wouldn't tell her things are going to work out if she was just going to a dinner meeting. What's going on?"

"Okay. I guess you ought to know anyway. The school

superintendent has asked her to appear before the school board to answer some questions."

"What for? Is she in trouble at school?"

Gram dunked a tea bag in her cup. "I don't know. A few days ago I thought this whole Crusade thing was silly. I was sure it would just blow away like so much hot air. Now I think we better be ready for a major storm."

I laughed. "That's good, Gram, a Major storm."

But when Gram didn't even crack a smile, I knew it was serious. My stomach tightened like it does when you're expecting a punch.

11

Wednesday morning I'd forgotten all about Mom's meeting with the school board. I didn't mean to, but mornings at our house aren't set up for much conversation. We've only got one bathroom, and if anyone gets out of step, it wrecks the whole routine. Anyway I grabbed my bike and left the house early. I didn't stop to pick up Buzz because I had to see the coach alone.

Mr. Huntley was in the phys. ed. office, his feet up on his desk, reading the paper and drinking coffee from a plastic cup. I said the right things and apologized for unsportsmanlike conduct. He liked that. And then I looked him right in the eye and promised not to let the team down again. I meant it, too.

He grunted something, but he leaned across the desk and shook my hand. "Okay. But if I ever see anything like that again, you're out, and that's a promise. Finished. Understood?"

"Yes, sir."

He picked up his newspaper and I knew he was through with me, except for one last shot. "Don't be late for practice."

"Today?"

"No, Troy, next year." He shook his head like he was dealing with Denny Dimwit. "Yes, today. The last meet's Saturday. You need all the practice you can get. Now get out of here."

"All right!" I was riding high. A great day, so far.

Later, on the way to English, I told Buzz, "I'm back on the team. Saw the coach this morning."

"Great. Did he give you a hard time?"

"Naw. The usual lecture. So, what happened yesterday?" I asked Buzz. "In English. Did Mrs. Lester hit the ceiling when I didn't show up?"

Buzz laughed. "You got it. But that didn't stop her. She gave us a quiz instead. The guys love you. You'll have to take a make-up test."

"Welcome back, Luther," Mrs. Lester said after the bell rang. "We missed your book review yesterday, so we'll get on with it today. You can take your make-up test after school."

"I've got swim practice."

"We'll discuss it after class. Tests certainly come before sports, but perhaps you can take it tomorrow. Now, as you may recall, we were trying to define censorship, and whether anyone has the right to decide what another person will read, write, or listen to. Did any of you discuss this at home?"

Esther Cotter sits right in front of me, and she was waving her hand until I thought it would fall off. Esther is such a creep. She knows everything, and I mean everything. Even when she gets an answer wrong, she acts like the teacher doesn't know what she's talking about. I could see Mrs. Lester was trying to ignore her, but finally she gave in.

"What is it, Esther?"

Old Esther stood up and checked to see if everyone was watching. "Mrs. Lester, I have to be excused from class."

Mrs. Lester gave one of her exaggerated sighs that we all knew meant, Oh what did I do to deserve this? "Are you ill, Esther?"

"No, Mrs. Lester, you don't understand." Esther plowed right on. She turned to fix her beady little eyes on me. "My father says he will not allow me to be present if we are going to discuss Mrs. Troy's book in class."

Mrs. Lester gasped, and I mean really gasped like a gaffed fish. "Well, my dear, really," she floundered.

I got to give Esther that, she knows how to get attention. Boy, you could have heard a cotton ball drop. I slid down in my seat. Something more was coming, I could feel it.

"My father says it's not right to allow books of that kind in school," she announced like she was the principal.

That lifted me right off my feet. "Hold it," I hollered. "What'd you mean? Books of what kind?"

Esther smirked, a really stupid look. "My father says people like your mother do not have the same values we do."

"Oh geez," I groaned. I wanted to choke her. "What the hell are you talking about, Esther?"

Mrs. Lester whapped her ruler. "Now Luther, relax. We will not have rude language in this classroom. Both of you sit down. She took a deep breath before she said, "What *are* you talking about, Esther? Perhaps you can explain what your father means."

"Yeah, let's talk about it," I said. "Did you read my mother's book, Esther? Or are you still reading *Bambi*?"

"That's enough!" Mrs. Lester gave me a her last-straw look. She walked around to the front of her desk. "But I think you're right, Luke. Let's talk about it now. We'll begin with your book report on *The Passionate Pirate*."

"The book report?" I was hoping she'd forget it.

"Yes," Mrs. Lester said. "You do remember the assignment, don't you? You did read the book?"

"I sure did. Yes, I read the book."

She raised her eyebrows and motioned to the front of the room. "Well then, let's hear it."

"Let's hear it," I repeated. "But I. . . ."

"But what?"

I had a brainstorm. "But I don't have my notes." That was no lie. I didn't have any notes at all. I hadn't even thought about taking notes while I'd been reading the book.

Mrs. Lester sighed. "Perhaps you can ad lib it, Luke. I'm sure you know the story well enough to summarize it for us." She swept her arm toward the front of the room like an usher. "Now, if you don't mind," she said.

There was no way out. As soon as I stood up Esther gathered her books and stalked out of the room. She didn't even wait for a pass or permission. "Does anyone else have an objection?" Mrs. Lester asked. Eddie Baxter shifted in his seat, but he stayed put.

I cleared my throat. "Well, *The Passionate Pirate* by my mother, I mean by Antonia Tyson, is about a guy, I mean the captain of a clipper ship. It happens before the Civil War, and it's about slavery and everything, and what I mean is this guy is, um. . . ." I cleared my throat again.

"Why is it called *The Passionate Pirate,* Luke?" Mrs. Lester asked. "Perhaps you can start with that."

"Well, you see this guy, his name is Matthew Hull, well he really, I mean the passionate part is because he cares so much about what he's doing."

I'd forgotten how much I hated oral reports, and how dumb they sound unless you can read them. I was trying to think what to say next when Mrs. Lester asked me, "Did you like the book?"

"Oh yeah, sure. It's a great story."

Then Mrs. Lester threw me a curve. "Would you have read it if it hadn't been your mother's book?"

I stood there with my mouth open for a second. "Gee, I don't know."

"Honestly, would you have read it?" she prodded me.

She'd said honestly, so I admitted, "I guess not. But not because of what it's about or anything like that. It's just that I don't like to read about romance and love and that stuff."

In an instant the room was a field of waving arms, but Eddie didn't wait for Mrs. Lester to call on him. "So how come it's got a sexy cover if it's such a great book?" he hollered. "And how come if your mother wanted to tell about slavery she wrote a book like that?"

"'Cause she wanted to!" I yelled at him. "And because

nobody'd read a regular kind of school book about this guy."

Suddenly everybody was talking at once, and in a flash I knew that good old Esther hadn't been so dumb. I wasn't going to stand there one more second and defend what my mother did. I mean, what the heck, did Buzz have to defend how his dad sells cars? I headed for the door, just like Esther.

News in our school travels as fast as the flu. All day kids hassled me about walking out of class, and guessed how many nights detention I was going to get. I still had to take the make-up test, but I could do that in detention. The only problem was, would the coach let me swim if he knew I had detention?

Things didn't look up until after school. Swim practice was great, except for Baxter who kept needling me until Buzz threatened to shove his head in a locker. Everyone was up for the Riverdale meet, the last one of the season. Riverdale kids think they're solid gold just because they've got an Olympic-size pool and even a separate diving pool. Big deal. We always work harder to beat them, especially when they come to our old tub, just to show them they're not so great. After practice I headed home alone.

If it hadn't been for the tulips and new green leaves on the trees, it would have been easy to think it was fall with election day coming up. I'd never seen so many posters and signs. They were nailed on every telephone pole and stuck on front lawns. Some advertised the rally with pictures of the Major and some had slogans against censorship, but all of them were printed in the world's brightest red, white, and blue. It looked like a draw, about half for and half against. The town was lining up, taking sides.

When I got home I almost tripped over Maggie sorting a pile of books in the garage right in front of my bike rack. She'd pick up a book, stare at the cover for a second and then plop it down on one pile. I watched her for a minute while she decided to put another book on a different pile.

"What the heck are you doing? Does Mom know you've got all this junk out here?"

"It's not junk. It's important."

"Who says?"

"Melissa's mommy. She said it's important to sort out our books and records."

"Why? She having a garage sale?"

"No. She just says we have to sort out good books and bad books."

"That's stupid. You haven't got any bad books."

"Melissa's mommy says we should get rid of questionable books, and I asked Grammy and she says questionable means you don't know for sure if something's good or bad."

"Does Mom know you're doing this?"

Maggie shook her head. Her bottom lip was quivering. "I just wanted to help." She sniffed and wiped her eyes with the back of her hand.

"Come on, Maggie. Everything's going to be okay." I felt sorry for the Maggot. She didn't have any idea of what was going on. I picked up *Mary Poppins* and a book about Ramona and a copy of *Winnie the Pooh*. "You don't have to get rid of any books, but don't bother Mommy, okay? I'll help you."

I found an empty carton in the corner of the garage. "Here. Put all your books in here and I'll carry them up to your room later. All right?"

"Okay, Luke. I really love all my books. I'm glad I don't have to throw them away."

Poor kid. It must be rough to be seven and not know what grownups were talking about. I hugged Maggie. She hugged me back, and in the blink of an eye, she was dancing around, back to her old self. "Know what? Mommy said I can watch you swim next time."

"That's great," I told her, "but remember. This is a secret. Don't say anything to Mom about throwing away any books, promise?"

Maggie nodded. "Promise," she said and crossed her heart.

Mom was in the kitchen frying chicken, and I could smell Gram's freshly baked bread. Guilt day, I call it; after Mom's been out for dinner, the next day we eat great.

"Hi, honey. How was school?" Mom asked.

"Okay. I talked to the coach. No problem." I didn't say anything about walking out of class. If Mom had heard it from Mrs. Lester already, I knew she'd bring it up.

But all she said was, "That's nice, dear. Will you switch on the news, please? My hands are greasy."

The newslady was talking about plans for some new kind of missile. "Wash your hands and set the table, will you Luke?" Mom asked me.

"Sure." For a meal like this, I'd do anything. Mom was carrying in the platter of chicken when the newslady said,

"And in the local news, protestors continued their vigil in front of the central school complex." They showed the people marching around the flagpole, with a close-up of the signs. Mom set down the platter, and muttered something under her breath.

Gram said, "Wouldn't you think they'd find something else to talk about?"

"At issue," the reporter was saying like she was announcing nuclear war, "is the use of the locally authored book, *The Passionate Pirate*, in a high school history course. The committee for the Crusade for a Clean America base their criticism on the book's vulgar language and explicit sexual episodes."

"Vulgar language?" Gram exploded. "Why, that's ridiculous. Don't they ever watch television? Or go to the movies? Now there's vulgar language! And usually no reason for it, either."

"Yeah, I didn't think it was so bad," I said. "I mean if that's how those slave traders talked, that's how you'd have to write it? Right?"

Mom raised one eyebrow, her "are you kidding?" look. She held up a hand. "Wait. Let me hear the rest of this."

". . . and a spokesman for the school board said that no decision would be announced until further investigation. And speaking of. . . ." Mom leaned over to turn off the television.

"Dinner's ready," she called to Maggie. She pulled out her chair, waited until we were all seated, and passed the chicken. Then she asked me, "So, you really read the book?"

12

That night I had a hard time getting to sleep. I wanted it to be next week. I wanted all this hassle about books and my mother to be over. I'd been thinking off and on about what it would be like living with my dad, even though I didn't really know him. It was the darnedest feeling, but I couldn't shake it.

Everywhere I went, there was some reminder of this dumb Crusade. The Major's picture was plastered on every post, and in every store window. You couldn't pick up the newspaper without seeing a picture of the Major speaking at Rotary and Kiwanis and every other club and church in town. Sometimes when I heard my Mom's name mentioned, I wanted to hide, and other times I wanted to grab people and make them listen to the story of Matthew Hull so they'd know Mom's book wasn't bad or dirty.

But most of all, I was really worried about the swim meet. I was scared about what might happen when my name was called for my event, or when I got on the starting block. What if I blew it again? Maybe I should tell the coach I couldn't handle the pressure, and that I couldn't swim. At least then if we lost, it wouldn't be my fault.

I woke up once in the middle of the night from a dream that seemed so real I was sure I smelled the chlorine. It had been a jumble of things, slaves in chains, and Mrs. Baxter waving my mother's book and chasing a pirate around the school pool, and me diving off the rail of a clipper ship into the ocean. Crazy!

Before I left for school Thursday morning, Gram cornered me. "Are you all right? I know that phone call upset you last night." She frowned. "It's not the first. I've answered a few, but I haven't told your mother. I don't know if she's had any. She probably wouldn't tell us if she did."

"I'm fine, Gram." I didn't feel fine, but if she was pretending, I figured I could, too. "No big deal. It'll all be over after the rally tomorrow, right?"

"Right." Gram hugged me extra hard. "Don't forget your lunch. I packed four brownies for dessert."

At school the pickets were still circling the flagpole like windup robots. Everybody else acted like they always did. I wondered if I looked the same. Funny how you can be churning up inside and nobody knows. I tried to think of a good excuse to get out of English, but I couldn't.

I wished I'd told my mother about walking out of Mrs. Lester's class. She'd probably hear about it soon, but I'd face Mom when the time came. First I had to find out what Mrs. Lester had in store for me.

Someone told me once that the best defense was a strong offense, or maybe it was the other way around, but anyway I went first. "I'm sorry, Mrs. Lester," I said as soon as I got to class. "I don't know what got into me yesterday. I shouldn't have walked out like that."

Mrs. Lester's offense was better. "I accept your apology, Luther, and I do understand how you feel," she said. "But I'm sending you to detention for two nights."

"Two nights?" I couldn't believe it. Guys did things ten times as bad and pulled one night.

Mrs. Lester didn't back down, but she did say, "I'll let you postpone it until next week, after the last swim meet. And you can take the make-up Monday morning. Is that clear?"

After I nodded yes, she told me to take my seat and then she started class. "As you can see," she announced, "I've put some different kinds of books on display, everything from *The American Heritage Dictionary* to *Charlotte's Web*. But they all have something in common. Who can tell me what it is?"

Someone said, "Same publisher?"

Mrs. Lester said, "No, look at them again."

I saw *The Diary of Anne Frank* and a couple of books by Judy Blume next to *Huckleberry Finn*. Kids guessed they all had the same binding, or the same author, or that they were all written in America, but none of these was the right answer. Finally Mrs. Lester zeroed in on me. "What do these books have in common, Luke?"

Why me? How come I was the expert all of a sudden? Then it dawned on me. "I get it. They were all censored or banned, right?"

"Aw, come on," Sikorski said. *"Charlotte's Web?* Give me a break."

"That can't be true. I've read every Judy Blume book," Mary Alice announced. "And my mother wouldn't let me read them if they weren't good."

"Luke is right, unfortunately," Mrs. Lester said. "Each of these books has been removed from a library or school reading list at one time or another. Of course we all know there is no such thing as a perfect book. . . ."

When she said that, Eddie raised his hand. "You're wrong. The Bible's perfect. Right?"

"But which version of the Bible?" Mrs. Lester asked.

Eddie sat up straight and pulled in his long legs under his desk. "What do you mean, version? There's only one Bible."

"Really?" Mrs. Lester sounded like she'd been waiting to spring this one. "Here's a copy of the *Good News Bible,* and here's the more traditional King James version, and this is the *New English Bible.*"

"We're Catholic," Bess interrupted. "I think our Bible is different from those."

Mrs. Lester agreed. "Yes, there are several Catholic versions as well. And each religion has its own equivalent of the Bible. Here is the Koran, the sacred text of the Islamic religion."

"Yeah, and my grandpa is Buddhist," a kid near the window said, "and his book's different, too."

"Okay, okay," Eddie said. "So what? There's nothing wrong with every church having its own kind of Bible. Big deal."

"The fact remains that there is no one book for all people, and that's fine," Mrs. Lester said. "We ought to be able to choose what we want to read."

Sikorski was waving his hand. "Hey, you're wrong. I know one book that's perfect, the dictionary. There's nothing wrong with that because it's just words."

Mrs. Lester looked like a comedian who'd just been handed the perfect straight line. *"The American Heritage Dictionary* is presently banned in some classrooms in six states," she said.

"Aw, come on. What for?" I couldn't believe this. She had to be exaggerating.

"They say it contains thirteen 'inappropriate' words," Mrs. Lester said.

"What's that mean? Dirty?" someone called.

"Who gets to find the words?" I think that was Sikorski, and everyone laughed.

Mrs. Lester picked up *The Diary of Anne Frank.* "Some of you read this last year. But it's been banned in some schools because it promotes religious tolerance."

"I thought that's supposed to be good — religious tolerance, I mean," I said.

"It is good, Luke. Our school committee urges you to read about Anne Frank in order to understand what happened to the Jewish people of Europe in those terrible years. And I think that's why Mrs. Troy wrote her book, too. Even though it's fiction, Mrs. Troy's book helps her history students understand one aspect of life during the days of slavery."

I looked around to see if Esther was listening to this, but she hadn't come to class. Too bad. It flashed through my mind that old Esther probably wouldn't get detention for walking out. She'd have a note from her parents.

Jennifer raised her hand. "But why did anyone want to ban *Charlotte's Web*? I love that book. It makes me cry every time I read it."

A couple of kids laughed, but I knew what she meant.

Mrs. Lester said, "Some people think children will get an unrealistic view of life from reading fantasy, and that certainly includes talking spiders." When everyone in the room started talking, Mrs. Lester held up her hand. "Do you think perhaps books are banned as a way of controlling what people think?"

"Hey, wait a minute," Eddie jumped in again. "Nobody's trying to control anyone. And not think? That's crazy. My mother's always telling people to think."

"Especially you," Buzz muttered.

I laughed, and Eddie leaned across the aisle to grab me. But I ducked and he missed. "I wouldn't laugh if I were you, Troy," he whispered.

"What's that supposed to mean?" I whispered back.

"My mother's on the right side. You guys are the ones in trouble."

I think I know how a bull feels when it sees the red cape waving. "You jerk!" I lunged out of my seat and practically sailed across the aisle, but I tripped over Baxter's long legs sticking out and whapped my arm on his desk. He grabbed my hand and twisted. I yelped and swung with my free arm, but it only caught him on the shoulder. I felt a yank on my shirt.

Buzz was shouting at me. "Troy! Knock it off." Someone else was trying to get between Eddie and me, and I almost socked Mrs. Lester in the jaw before I realized who it was.

I was puffing and heaving, and adrenaline was still charging through me, but I sat down. It got real quiet, like everybody was waiting for lightning to strike. It did. Mrs.

Lester's words were almost a whisper, but they came across loud and clear. "Edward and Luther. I will not tolerate fighting in my classroom. You are suspended. I want you out!"

I didn't even care. Fine with me. If I never came back into that room again, it would be too soon.

It seemed like an hour before anyone moved or talked, and then it was Buzz. "You can't do that Mrs. Lester. Not suspension!"

Mrs. Lester glared at him. She seemed surprised that anyone would question her order. "And why not?"

"Suspension means they'd be off the team. The Riverdale meet's on Saturday. It's the last one. The coach'll throw a fit," Buzz told her. "And without Luke and Eddie, we'll lose for sure."

Eddie unfolded like a Swiss Army knife, and when he stood up he was eye to eye with Mrs. Lester. "Yeah," he said, "I mean yes, ma'am, Buzz's right. We've got to be there. Please?"

Then it sunk in. Suspension. But it wouldn't matter about the swim meet because I'd be dead. My mother'd kill me.

Mrs. Lester looked from Eddie to me and back again a couple of times. Finally she cleared her throat and shook her head. "No, I want you out. There's enough tension without you two fighting. Do not come to class tomorrow, and on Monday we'll meet with your guidance counselors to decide whether or not this is a suspendable offense. Is that clear?"

It couldn't be any clearer if she'd injected it directly into our brains. I was afraid to open my mouth. I was facing two nights of detention already, and maybe suspension. I didn't want to try for more, so I was glad when Eddie said, "Yes ma'am, but where should we report tomorrow during English period?"

"Study hall," she said. "You can work on your debate projects. You do remember the projects that are due at the end of the marking period, don't you?"

"Oh no," I mumbled, but Mrs. Lester heard me.

"Is there a problem, Mr. Troy?"

"No, Mrs. Lester, no problem," I said real quick. It wasn't a problem; it was a major catastrophe. And I'd forgotten all about it. Early in the semester, way back before we'd even heard of the Major or his Crusade, we'd drawn names out of a hat for debate partners, and mine was Eddie Baxter.

13

Friday. The big Friday of the rally was finally here. When my alarm buzzed, I slapped it off, turned over, and put the pillow over my head. Nuts. Why didn't I just run away? I knew I couldn't fake anything sick enough to stay home again, not and still get out of the house after school. And if I headed for school and cut out before the first bell, where would I go? In this town, someone would spot me and it'd get back to Mom faster than the speed of light.

"Face it, Troy," I told the bathroom mirror. "Just get through it. All this fuss can't last forever."

When Mom dropped me off in front of the junior high she said, "Do you have swim practice after school, dear?"

"A short one," I told her. "Why?"

"I'd like you to get home as soon as you can. I'll need your help. We have to get the signs loaded in the car."

"Yeah, for the rally." When there's no way out, you might as well roll with it. "Okay, Mom. See you later."

Before I shut the car door, Mom leaned across the seat.

"Don't look so glum. The sun's shining. It's going to be a great day."

"Oh sure, Mom." Big deal, the sun was shining. The way I felt, it might as well have been a total eclipse.

In homeroom I kept my head in a book, pretending I was finishing the math assignment until the bell rang and we had to salute the flag and listen to announcements and take attendance. Then I managed to fade into the background long enough to make it to English period without any hassles, and I even headed toward the big study hall. But I didn't go in. I kept right on walking, and my feet seemed to take me down to the pool locker room. I lucked out. It was empty and dark. It must have been the coach's free period.

I flopped down on a bench with my books as a pillow, and closed my eyes. It was good to be alone and quiet, but it didn't last long. Suddenly the lights came on and I heard voices. One was the coach saying, "Take it easy, son. Listen, there are times when you just have to roll with life."

The other voice said, "But it's messing up everything. How much can a guy take?" It was Eddie.

I sat up, picked up my books, and hoped I could make my escape without them seeing me. I could see the coach in his office with his arm around Eddie. They were facing away from me, and I was only two steps from the locker room door, when the coach said, "It's not easy for Luke either, you know. You boys are up against a hard lesson."

I could feel a lecture coming, and my hand was on the doorknob, ready to get out of there, when the coach said,

"It's the easiest thing in the world to talk big about your principles, until it gets personal. That's when you decide how much an idea means to you, and if it's worth defending."

Eddie said, "But what if it's not even a guy's own idea? Why'd my mother have to drag me into her fight?"

"That's a problem," the coach admitted and then he said something about being friends even if you disagree, and that's when I left.

*

The day dragged like a boulder on a rope. I didn't talk much to anyone except Buzz. "What's with you?" he must have asked me twenty times, but I couldn't tell him. Everything was with me, like it was piled on my shoulders — two nights detention ahead, a meeting with a guidance counselor to see if I'd be suspended, a big swim meet that I might mess up again, and a dumb debate project I hadn't thought about since it was assigned. I didn't have any idea how I'd pull that off. How do you plan a debate with a guy you're not even talking to? And the thing that made me really mad was that none of this would have happened if my mom hadn't written that book or if the Major had stayed out of our town. Geez, none of it was my fault!

After school at swim practice I kept out of Eddie's way, and I only talked to Buzz for a minute when he asked me to go to the rally with him. It felt like the longest day of my life, and the last thing I needed to see when I got home was half the town parked in our driveway. I met Mom coming down the back steps, lugging a big box.

"Hi, dear. You're just in time." I took the box from her. It was heavier than it looked. "Put it in the back of the station wagon, will you, please?" Mom said. "Have a snack, and then you can help us get the car loaded. Thanks, dear." She patted my cheek and hurried back into the house.

I don't know how long it took us, but we piled signs and boxes of pamphlets into the back of our old wagon until it looked like the last stop on a paper drive. Gram was zinging around so fast, I was surprised she wasn't wearing her roller skates. She was everywhere at once, directing the ladies from the senior center like an admiral with her fleet. The old women were all wearing their slogan sweatshirts. Gram's bright blue one said "Aged to Perfection," and a skinny little lady was almost drowning in a huge red shirt that read "Don't Trust Anyone Under 60."

Jez wasn't milling around chasing her tail and barking, which seemed strange. Mom said Maggie was dog-sitting, and I found them both in Maggie's bedroom. Jez was moping on the bed, wrapped in a faded pink blanket and wearing a baby bonnet that almost covered her eyes. She thumped her tail when she heard me and struggled to get her paws untangled from doll clothes. Maggie said, "Luuuke, leave her alone. She's my baby."

I hugged Jez and patted her. She looked at me with sad eyes, like I was a traitor. "It's okay, girl. Maggie's taking care of you. That's a good dog." I wished I could trade places with her.

Maggie tucked the blanket around Jez. "Mommy says I can stay at Laurie's house tonight."

"That's nice." At least I wouldn't have to babysit. I pulled Maggie's door shut and almost made it to my room when Mom called me again.

"Luke, can you come down, please?" And I was off on more errands. The last one was to order enough pizza to feed everyone still helping.

Later, while we were eating, I heard Mom tell a couple of women, "Luke will unload the signs and you can hand them out as people arrive at the rally."

"But I'm going with Buzz, Mom."

"Oh, I'm sorry dear, but I need you, just for a little while. I really do. Call Buzz and tell him you'll meet him there."

I shrugged and let it pass. No point in stirring up more trouble. It'd be over soon. Mom drove with me and Gram squeezed in the front seat of the loaded station wagon. She pulled in behind the Grange hall and backed into a space along the driveway. "This looks good," she said. "Luke, you can take the signs out of the back and lean them against that tree."

The signs had jostled around in the car until they looked like a pile of uncooked spaghetti. I was pulling a bunch of them out when I felt a jab in my back so hard I dropped the signs. "Hey, watch it," I yelled.

I swung around and collided with Eddie Baxter who was carrying a stack of signs from his mother's van. "Baxter, you idiot! Watch where you're going. Look what you made me do."

"I made you do? You bumped into me. And if I get mud on these signs my mother will kill me," Eddie yelled back.

"Good. I'll help her." I turned to pick up our signs and Eddie scooped up theirs.

When a man stopped to ask Eddie for a sign, I heard Eddie tell him, "Thanks, Mr. Cavaleri. Have a good time."

Good time? That did it. I grabbed one of Mom's signs and practically shoved it into the hands of a woman passing by. "Take a sign," I told her. "Have a good time." She looked at me like I was nuts, but she took it.

Mrs. Baxter called, "Follow me, Edward. Bring that box of pamphlets, and put on your hat." She handed him one of the white plastic Crusade hats. I watched Eddie trot after his mother like a good doggie. When my Mom called a few seconds later, I found myself doing the same thing.

I kept an eye out for Buzz and the other guys. Finally I saw them heading my way. "I'm going now, Mom. See you later."

"Okay dear. Thanks for the help."

The park was full of people. I caught up with Buzz and Sikorski. Buzz stuffed a fresh lump of bubble gum in his mouth and mumbled something like, "Whatchathink?"

"About what?" Sikorski could always translate Buzz's mumbles.

Buzz flapped his arms at the crowd. "All this stuff. The rally. My mom says its creepy. She didn't want to come, but Dad said she had to."

"Boy, my mom's here with a whole gang of people," I said. "They've been working on this like it was a presidential campaign."

Buzz blew a bubble as big as his face and gunked it back into his mouth in one smooth swipe. "Yeah, and she's not the only one. Look at that bunch."

A group of people wearing the white Crusade hats marched in waving signs that said stuff like "Clean Books for Clean Minds." Buzz slapped my back. "Fireworks, Troy. I can feel it. Excitement in the old town tonight."

I felt it, too, but it wasn't a good feeling. We followed the crowd onto the field. We didn't just amble along like we were going to the firemens' picnic — we were practically marching. It was hard not to with trumpets blaring and drums beating out of the loudspeakers. There couldn't have been many people sitting home tonight. Our neighbor, Mrs. Kramer, hustled by with a couple of other ladies. She waved. I almost didn't recognize her without her broom.

We saw people carrying shopping bags and boxes full of books and records. A few had only one book or magazine, but most came empty-handed, like maybe they just wanted to see what the rally was all about.

A big rig the size of a moving van was parked at the far end of the field. One side had been folded down on legs so it became a stage. Tons of red, white, and blue cloth were draped around it, and dozens of tiny American flags fluttered in a line along the footlights. A spotlight danced over a banner above the stage that said "Rally for Purity . . . Clean Up America" in huge letters. Off to the right of the stage five men were piling up wood for a bonfire. A couple of television crews were laying cables and tripping over each other trying to find the best place to film the whole thing.

It looked like a football pep rally but it didn't feel like one. A lot of people stared straight ahead or nodded to each other, but they didn't say much. They acted as though they weren't really sure if they should be there or not. The sky had darkened and it was hard to see faces unless you were standing near one of the spotlights.

"Weird." Buzz started to say something else, but he was drowned out by the roar of cheers and clapping. "Hey, it's the Major. Come on, let's get closer."

14

Buzz slipped through the crowd like an eel through seaweed, and Sikorski and I followed. "Coming through," Buzz'd say like he was an official, and people stepped back before they realized it was just kids. We worked our way up front and over to the left side of the stage where my mom's friends were waving their signs. Up close like that we could see three pyramids of the Major's book piled on the stage just behind the footlights. He certainly knew how to sell stuff.

When I saw Gram, I moved up next to her. She was holding a sign that said "Hitler Burned Books. Not in America." "Great sign," I said. "But no one's going to burn books, right?"

She shrugged. "Let's hope not."

The loudspeaker hanging in the tree right next to us blasted, "Ladies and gentlemen, boys and girls, welcome." Gradually the talking stopped as one person poked another and pointed to the stage. Finally it was quiet.

One of the white-hatted Crusaders threw some kerosene on the bonfire, and when he lit it the flames burst up in such a loud "whoosh" that people stepped back and said, "Ahhh," like they do on the Fourth of July. The wood crackled and popped. Long red and orange flames licked the dry old two-by-fours and reached for the top of the pile. It was like being at a giant campfire, sort of soothing and hypnotizing when you stared at it.

The Major's white jacket gleamed in the spotlight. "Great outfit," Buzz said. "Nice touch with the red vest and blue slacks."

"Dear friends, this is an evening to remember." The Major's voice flowed like glue and everyone seemed stuck on it. "Our Crusade is a momentous event in your town and in your personal lives. Tonight you will reclaim the goodness and purity that forged this nation to greatness."

It sounded good even to me, and I didn't like the guy. There was something about his voice and the way he looked so sincere that made you want to believe him. "Tonight," the Major boomed on, "you and your neighbors will pledge hearts and minds to homes, schools, and libraries free of the subversive filth that weakens our nation and. . . ."

From way back in the crowd a voice bellowed, "*Boo-o-o-o!* We have free speech in this nation." Everyone turned to look, like iron filings following a magnet. Here and there signs waved. A few more "Hitler Burned Books" signs appeared and Gram hoisted hers higher.

Someone must have turned up the amplifier then because the Major's voice thundered over the noise. "Silence! Silence! Kindly hear me out, dear friends. Of course you are free to choose, and I am confident that you will choose our course . . . clean minds and clean books." A cheer rumbled through the crowd.

The Major said a lot more, but I tuned him out and watched the fire until suddenly he dropped his voice to a lower pitch, like a TV salesman warning you this was the last day of the sale. "I can see that many of you have brought books and video tapes with you," the Major said softly into the microphone. He waited a second until the whole field was quiet before he went on. "Right now, dear friends, please bring them forward and place them on the stage as an act of cleansing."

A woman walked carefully around the fire, her shadow like a stalking monster as she lifted a stack of books and set them at the Major's feet.

Gram huffed, "She's on his committee."

"Thank you, dear lady," the Major shouted, and then he looked over the crowd again and circled his arms like he was gathering everyone in. "Come forward, don't hesitate. Let this be your outward symbol of commitment to our cause. Please join me in singing that great hymn, 'God Bless America' while you come forward."

He signaled backstage and a tape blasted out the song. Several people went up to put books or tapes on the stage. A few people around us began to sing; with that kind of rousing music, it was hard not to. Then more and more joined in, but even so, it was slow going, and the Major rubbed his hands together as though that might speed things up. "Come forward, dear friends," he called again. Then he covered his lapel microphone with one hand and leaned over to whisper to one of his aides.

At the end of the second verse, I saw the Major's man jump from the stage and speak to a man in the front row of people. A few seconds later that man rose from his seat, a stack of records in his arms. But instead of putting the albums on the stage, he strode over to the fire, hesitated for a moment, and then heaved the records into the flames. The album jackets crackled, and bits of colored paper flew up and danced in the hot air. Black smoke puffed out from the melting plastic, and boy did it stink!

It took a second or two for word of what the man had done to ripple through the crowd. A woman ran up next and threw two books into the blaze. My mother went crazy. She yelled, "No, no! Don't burn them!" but nobody listened. The Major had stepped back out of the spotlight. He watched a few more people dump books into the fire, but he didn't say anything. We wouldn't have heard him anyway over the screams and shouts that blended into a roar without words.

Suddenly I saw Eddie and Mrs. Baxter towering over everyone like grownups at a kids' party. Eddie's mother was struggling to push through the crowd, and it looked like Eddie was trying to hold her back. Maybe she'd embarrassed him enough, and for half a second I felt sorry for him. Eddie was arguing with her and trying to hang on to her, but Mrs. Baxter broke away. With a bunch of books cradled in one arm like a football, she straight-armed a man who blocked her way, and charged through the line better than our high school quarterback. And all the time Eddie was hollering, "No, Ma. Stop!"

But she just kept going, leaving Eddie behind. She waved one of the paperback books over her head before she pitched it into the blaze. Someone grabbed Mrs. Baxter's arm and when she spun around, books scattered in the dirt. I could see the cover in the firelight. It was a lady in a lowcut dress and a pirate was hugging her. Mom's book!

I thought my blood was going to boil right out of me. I headed straight for Mrs. Baxter, but Mom practically threw a body block when she dropped her sign and grabbed me. "Luke, stop! No fighting."

"Let me go. She can't do that," I screamed. I pulled one arm free but Mom was hanging on for dear life. Then Gram made her big move.

Before anyone could stop her, Gram darted to the stage and snatched one of the Major's books from the stack behind the footlights. She shoved through the Crusaders who had clustered around Mrs. Baxter. "Two can play this game," Gram shouted, and I saw the Major's book sail into the flames.

For a second, everyone froze, but the rest happened faster than it takes to tell about it. The Major leaped off the stage and landed with a splat between Gram and the fire. Gram went sprawling, and a bunch of people behind her fell down like dominoes. She yelped, and scrambled to her feet, both arms swinging. One of Gram's wild swings connected with the Major's jaw, but when he threw up his arms to protect himself, his flashy ring caught Gram on the cheek.

I broke away from Mom and charged in to help Gram. Right behind me I heard Buzz holler, "Geronimo," and Sikorski's crazy Tarzan yell. I heard Eddie screaming something, too, but I lost track of him when he disappeared under a mass of scrambling people.

Whistles blew. People screamed, "Police! Get the cops." But the cops were already moving in, tripping over cords and cables to get past the television crews who didn't want to miss one minute of the battle. Three Crusade guys swarmed around the Major. Two big men leaned over to help Gram up, but somehow they got tripped or shoved and fell into the heap, too.

Finally I bulldozed my way through the crowd until I caught an elbow smack in the eye that staggered me. For a second I really saw stars, just like they draw them in the comics. I blinked a couple of times before I could see Gram again, and even then she looked blurry to me.

It was hard to tell exactly what happened next because it was like one of those riots on the TV news where all you see are people's backs and their arms flailing around. By the time I got to Gram, an officer was reading from a card, "You have the right to remain silent. . . ."

"Me?" Gram sobbed. The officer clicked handcuffs on her. "I was protecting my daughter's book, and . . . and what about the First Amendment?" Blood trickled down Gram's cheek, but with her hands cuffed, she couldn't even wipe it away.

Mom pushed her way through the people and reached for Gram just as the officer hustled her away. The crowd faded back, as though they didn't want to get involved now.

Another cop hefted the Major to his feet, read him his rights, and snapped handcuffs on him, too. Mrs. Baxter, streaked with dirt and her dress torn, hovered near the Major like a mother hen whose chick has been thrown in the soup.

Mom looked as scared as a little kid, but she lifted her chin, straightened her shoulders, and called to Gram, "Don't worry, Mother. I'll call a lawyer."

"Are you just going to let her go?" I couldn't believe it. Why didn't Mom tell that cop that Grandma hadn't done anything wrong? But Mom wasn't paying any attention to me. She gasped and put her hand over her mouth when she saw Gram stumble. Then the officer put his arm around Gram, and gently held his hand on her head so she wouldn't bump it as she got into the back seat of the squad car.

Major Madison was limping, but for once he was quiet. His face was as white as his jacket had been before it got smeared with mud and ashes. A policeman led him around the car and jammed him in next to Gram.

Before the officer closed the car door, Gram called to us, "I'm all right. Don't worry." But her chin trembled and all of a sudden she looked old and frail.

"They can't do this to you, Gram," I hollered. "We'll get you out."

Mom put her arm around me and we stood there like a couple of refugees from a tornado. I looked around for Buzz or Sikorski but everyone seemed to have scattered. The police car pulled away, red light whirling, and the television people searched around for someone to interview. A reporter hustled over to Mom and shoved a microphone in her face. "Aren't you Antonia Tyson? Can you tell us how you feel about your book causing the angry outburst we have witnessed here tonight?"

Mom's voice was like ice. "No," she said, and stalked off with me so close behind her we could have worn the same shoes. By the time we got to our parking place, most of the other cars had gone, except for the Baxters. Eddie's mother was perched on the ledge of the open van door and Eddie was pacing. Mrs. Baxter was crying, and Eddie looked as miserable as I felt.

I didn't say anything. I didn't expect I'd ever talk to Eddie again, but Mom walked over to them. "Edith? Are you all right?"

Mrs. Baxter wiped her face with a wad of rumpled Kleenex. She sniffed real loud and nodded. "Yes, thank you." Her voice was shaky. "Oh, Martha," she said before she choked on some new sobs. Finally she blew her nose and wiped her eyes again. "Martha, I didn't mean for this to happen. It all just, well, it got out of hand."

Mom nodded. "Yes, out of hand," she agreed. Her voice went up a notch, like it does when she's about to take charge. She reached for Mrs. Baxter's arm. "Come on, Edith. Let's go down to the police station and get this straightened out."

15

This town's police station is about the size of a gas station. When everyone's on duty there are only enough cops to go one-on-one with a basketball team. The county sheriff sends over a few extra officers when anything big comes up, which is maybe the Memorial Day parade, or when the governor stops to give a speech in an election year.

By the time we got there, the station was jammed. A tall skinny cop with a brand-new brush cut stood with his back against the double doors. Mom pushed. The skinny cop bounced forward a step, but he shoved back. He was busy calling, "Quiet folks, settle down," but nobody seemed to pay any attention.

Mom pushed the door again. "Excuse me," she said a couple of times before the officer turned around.

"What's your business?" He scowled, but he held the door open a crack. Mom put her foot, then her shoulder in. She smiled.

"Thank you, officer. My mother was brought in by mistake and I want to see her, please. This is my son." She put her arm around my shoulder. "And Mrs. Baxter and her son are with us."

"Yes ma'am. Right this way." The cop held the door wide and we became part of the mob inside. Mom was almost as good as Buzz at squeezing through a crowd. I grabbed onto the back of her jacket and charged in behind her with the Baxters stuck to me like Velcro patches.

The main room was a lot like the school office. Phones rang on the long counter along one side. As the four of us pushed through, I caught snatches of conversation. "But officer, I didn't do anything," and "Don't I get one phone call?" and "I'm not saying anything until my lawyer gets here." It sounded familiar, but maybe I was just remembering television cop shows.

While Mom tried to find out about Grandma, I worked my way down the counter toward a row of benches. And there was Gram. Wisps of white hair fell in her face. The blood had dried in a long streak down one cheek and splotched her sweatshirt. But from her expression, I could tell she was having a great time. I hadn't known what to expect, but I couldn't believe this.

"Gram! What's happening? I mean, are you okay?"

Gram beamed at me, one of her come-here-my-favorite-grandchild smiles. "Oh Luther. I'm so glad to see you. What a time we've had. Where's your mother?" Before I could answer, she held up her hand. It was smeared with ink.

"You've been fingerprinted! Wow!" I realized this was serious.

"Oh my yes, and mugged. I mean we had photos taken. And they've set bail."

"Bail? Holy cow. What did they charge you with?"

Gram shoved over on the bench and grabbed my arm. "Sit down, Luke. We may have to wait a while." She glanced at the man next to her. "Have you met Major Madison, dear? But of course you have."

It wasn't the same Major I'd seen before. This one looked like he'd been broken to private. His red vest had lost a few buttons, and one fat knee poked through a jagged rip in his muddy trousers. His jaw was swelling and turning blue. It looked like his hairspray had given up because white waves of hair hung in limp strands over his forehead, even though he kept pushing them back. He nodded and muttered something that I guessed was, "We've met."

Gram was wound tighter than her three dollar alarm clock. "The Major and I were having the most fascinating discussion, Luke. He's been telling me about his Crusade." Gram had a gleam in her eye that she gets when she's excited. "I was just going to ask him why he does this." She turned to the Major. "Why do you, Major?"

"Do what?" The Major mumbled. He didn't seem up to a discussion, fascinating or not.

Before Gram could tell him what, an officer appeared in front of us. "Ruth Wilson," he read from his clipboard, then he looked at Gram. "Are you Ruth Wilson?" When she nodded, he took her arm and said, "Come with me, please."

The Major stood up. "What about me? I insist on speaking to someone in authority immediately."

Gram patted the Major's shoulder. "Be patient. Your

turn will come. I'll be back soon, Luke." She looked up at the tall officer and asked him, "May I talk to my daughter? I'll need to see her, please."

I watched Gram scurry after the officer toward Mom, who was waiting by the long counter with the Baxters. Mom hugged Gram and then the two of them followed the policeman into an office.

The Major slumped back on the bench, wiped a hand over his face, and then suddenly slammed a fist on his knee. That made him wince, and he mumbled something under his breath.

"So, why do you do this?" I thought I might as well find out. This guy had caused me enough trouble to last until I was thirty. He owed me.

When the Major didn't answer, I asked again, "This Crusade thing. And my mom's book — you didn't even read it, did you? Why did you come to our town anyway? Was it just a publicity tour? To sell your book?"

That hit a nerve. The Major sat up like he'd been poked. "Young man, you are insolent and rude. I conduct my Crusade because it must be done. If I didn't believe so ardently in this cause, I would not subject myself to . . . to this monstrous abuse." He took in the whole police station with one sweeping wave of his hand. He was on a roll, and I was almost sorry I'd asked. "Do you think I just picked this town willy-nilly? No sir, the committee was formed by a group here, and it was they who invited me. I merely lent my prestige."

He brushed his hair back and stuck out his puffy chin. "If there is blame to be laid, young man, it is with people like your mother. Had she not chosen to subject her students to that unsavory book, some of your citizens might not have asked me to bring my Crusade here in the first place." He tugged at his red vest. "Well sir, there are other communities waiting for me. Our Crusade will not die just because of this outrageous action tonight. Other people in other places will hear our message. With all my heart and mind I believe we must monitor the ideas our young people. . . ."

That steamed me. "Hey, wait a minute. You don't think much of kids, do you? Don't you think we can sort out some things for ourselves? Don't you think we. . . ." Before I could finish, another officer stood in front of us.

"Major Madison?" he asked. He motioned to the Major. "Come with me, please?"

I followed them back through the crowd, which was thinning out. Mom and Gram were just coming out of the office as the Major went in.

"Thank you for paying my bill, Martha," Gram said. "They wouldn't take Mastercard."

"That's all right, Mother. Let's go." She put her arm around Gram's shoulder.

"I'll pay you back, dear. But fifty dollars does seem like a lot for disturbing the peace, which I certainly was not doing. That rally was not a bit peaceful, and I did no more than you would do to protect me, I'm sure."

"Mother, it's all right. Come on." Mom sounded tired.

"Just a minute." An officer shoved a clipboard toward Gram. "Sign here, please. I'll give you a copy, and you be sure to come back on the date it says there for your court appearance."

Gram signed the paper and handed the clipboard back.

"Yes sir, I'll do that. Thank you."

The officer tore off Gram's copy and gave it to her. "And in the future, Mrs. Wilson, stick to your knitting, or whatever you people do over there at the senior center."

I probably looked as surprised as Gram and Mom. I couldn't tell who was angrier, but had a feeling that one of them was about to explode. "Come on, Gram," I said. "Let's go home. He didn't mean anything."

Mom's mouth hung open and Gram sputtered. For once she was speechless, but the officer just went right on. "Keep an eye on her," he told Mom. And to make it worse, he winked.

Mom shot him a look known to wither any student. "Why of course, officer."

The officer smiled, but he'd missed the point of Mom's poison dart. "That's the trouble with mothers. You never can tell what they'll do next," he said with a little "heh-heh-heh" chuckle at the end.

I grabbed Mom and Gram and pushed them ahead of me toward the door. As we squeezed past the Baxters, who were still waiting for the Major, I heard Eddie mutter, "Yeah, mothers!"

16

When I woke up Saturday morning, I could hardly get my eyes unglued. And my legs were paralyzed from Jez sleeping on them. I shoved her off. "Come on you dumb dog, move."

The face that stared back at me from the mirror didn't look like mine. What a shiner! My eye was not only black, it was puffed out like I was hiding a baseball under my cheek. Who'd believe I had only run into an elbow?

I wandered downstairs, but didn't find anyone. The newspaper thwacked against the front door, and when I went to get it, Jez almost knocked me over in her hurry to get out. The front page of the paper had a huge picture of the mob at the rally. "Crusaders Clash" read the headline. It made the rally sound more like a football game. Maybe the sports editor wrote headlines on weekends.

The article went right to the point: "The Crusade for a Clean America, held Friday night in the park behind Grange hall, ended in a free-for-all scuffle among participants when an unknown person threw books into the bonfire. The conflict. . . ."

I didn't read anymore. It was over. I went upstairs, took

a shower, and when I got downstairs again, Mom was drinking coffee in the dining room.

"Morning, dear," she mumbled from the other side of the newspaper.

Gram came in from the kitchen with a platter of waffles. "Good morning, Luke," she said, but winced. "Ummm, it hurts to talk."

"Your cheek's turning black and blue, Gram. You feel okay?" I asked her.

She nodded, put the waffles on the table and pulled up a chair. "You don't look too spiffy yourself."

Mom laid down her paper. "Good heavens. I didn't realize you'd been hurt, Luke. Who socked you in the eye?"

"Who knows?" I reached for the waffles and syrup.

"I guess we can be grateful it wasn't worse." Mom took a big gulp of coffee, and shook her head. "You two. You should see yourselves. You look like leftovers from a prize fight."

"So what happens next?" I asked with my mouth full.

"Well, I have to go back for my hearing," Gram said. "But the nice officer told me the case will probably be dismissed because it's my first offense. I don't know what will happen to the Major, but he has to show up, too. We were both charged with disturbing the peace." She sighed. "I'm glad your grandfather wasn't around to see this. I can't believe I threw that book in the fire. I don't know what came over me, Martha. And I want to apologize. I'm deeply ashamed."

Mom patted Gram's hand. "That's all right, Mother. You were pretty riled up."

"But don't you see, dear. If a perfectly sensible person like me can get carried away like that, imagine what can happen to . . . well, it's frightening." Gram sipped her coffee. "The Major's very convincing, you know, and he really believes he's right."

"And who's going to stop him?" I asked. "I think the Major *wanted* people to burn books."

Gram raised her eyebrows. "Yes, as long as they weren't his books."

"You may be right, Luke." Mom helped herself to a waffle. "You know what? I think people are afraid."

"Of what?" I wanted to know. "The Major?"

"I'm not sure. Everything, I guess — drugs, AIDS, terrorism. . . ."

"And burning some books is going to fix those things?" I didn't buy that.

"Of course not. But there's an old saying that ignorance is bliss. Maybe people think that if their children don't know about the bad things, they won't be hurt by them," Mom said. "I wish I could protect you and Maggie from the evil in life, but I'd rather have you know how to make good choices."

I reached for another waffle. "You're getting gooey, Mom."

She laughed. "Heaven forbid."

"Well, gooey or not, I agree," Gram said. "But I've been around longer than either of you have, and I can tell you that ignorance is *not* bliss. It's far better to go through life with your eyes open."

"Which won't be easy for Luke," Mom said. "Do you really think you should swim tonight with your eye so

swollen? Maybe you and Gram should both see a doctor."
But before we got into that discussion, the phone rang.

"Get that, will you Luke? It's probably Maggie. I have to pick her up at Laurie's house." Mom was halfway up the stairs when she called down, "Tell her I'm getting dressed and I'll be right there."

But it was Buzz. "Hey, how're you doing? Heard you were in the lockup last night, Troy. Can you swim tonight?"

"Yeah, I'll swim. My gram was in jail, not me. But she's out on bail."

Buzz hooted. "No kidding, out on bail? Your grandma? That's wild." He laughed. "You're lucky Mrs. Lester didn't sentence you yet. I'll bet your mom hit the ceiling when she heard you might be suspended."

I looked to see if Mom was near the phone. She wasn't, but I kept my voice low anyway. "She doesn't know yet."

"She doesn't know? Boy, she'll ground you forever. My dad always leans on me harder if I don't tell him stuff like that right away."

"Yeah, I know. But with everybody bugging her about her book, well, I don't know. I just didn't. And anyway, she doesn't have to know until Monday. At least old Lester gave us time, and so far I don't think she's mentioned it to Mom."

"Maybe your luck's good on this one, Troy," Buzz said. "I hope it holds up tonight. We'll need all the luck we can find. The Riverdale team's tougher than Prescott."

"Right," I agreed. "So did you hang around the park after Gram got arrested or what?"

"For a little while. There were a few minor scuffles before they cleared the place out." Buzz laughed. "I landed in some gunk near the fire. Tar or something."

"So are you all right? I mean, can you swim tonight?"

"Oh yeah. Wouldn't miss it. But I have got a kind of problem."

"Like what?"

"You won't believe it till you see it. Hey, I gotta go. Mom's calling me. She's going to fix it now."

"Fix what?" But Buzz had hung up.

That afternoon Gram and I sat around with ice on our swollen faces, and we talked about Mom's book and the rally.

"So, do you think they'll let Mom keep on using her book in her history class? What did the school board decide?"

"Nothing yet. Decision pending." Gram shrugged. "Who knows what will happen now? I imagine the board will hold a public meeting. Talk is better than bonfires."

"I guess. But who decides the winner?"

Gram shifted the ice bag on her cheek. "I don't know that there are any winners. Honey, the older I get the less I understand people. I like to think that the whole point of education is to learn lots of different ideas so each person can choose what's right for himself." The hall clock chimed and Gram jumped up. "And what's right for me is to get ready for my date."

"You going out with Art Hastings again?"

"Oh my, no. But I met a lovely man at the center when we were painting signs. He's taking me to your swim meet — he's a retired coach. I've bragged about you, so you'd better be good."

"Sure, Gram. I just hope I can see the end of the pool."

Gram laughed. "Your eye is beginning to look remarkably like a pirate's patch. Rather black, but interesting."

Around five o'clock I had a big glass of orange juice and a sandwich. I knew there'd be a ton of food at Buzz's house after the meet. His parents had invited the team over to celebrate, win or lose.

Mom asked if I wanted a ride to school, but I told her I needed to walk. "Okay, dear. Good luck. And Luke, don't let anyone rattle you tonight."

"Rattle me?"

Mom smiled. "Yes, dear; Gram told me what happened at the Prescott swim meet." She smothered me in a huge hug. "That must have been awful. I wish you'd told me. I'm so sorry."

I pulled away from the hug. "You're sorry? I'm the one who goofed up. But it won't happen again, not after last night. What could rattle me after all that?"

She planted a kiss on my forehead and I didn't even duck. "I'm proud of you, Luke. I guess I haven't told you that lately, have I? I know it hasn't been easy for you without a dad and with me working. And I get so used to the way you and Maggie and Gram all help around here that sometimes I forget to tell you now much I appreciate it."

Why'd she have to say she was proud of me? She wouldn't be when she found out about detention and all that stuff. I could see her lean over for another kiss, but I slipped out of this one. "Heck, Mom, it's like you always said, we all live here, so we all help. No big deal."

"Well, anyway. . . ." Mom started to say something else, but I interrupted her because all of a sudden it felt like the right time for a true confession, and I blurted it out fast before the moment passed. "Listen, Mom," I said, "there's some stuff I ought to tell you."

"All right, dear. I'm listening."

"Well, it's just that I've been getting into a lot of fights lately and, gee, I don't know what's happening to me. Like with Eddie Baxter — I get so mad every time I see him that I want to belt him. And a couple of times in school. . . ."

Before I finished that part of the confession, Mom said, "I know about the detention, Luke. At least you only walked out of class. You didn't fight that time."

"You know? I don't believe this! All this time you knew? How come you didn't say anything? I can't believe you'd let me suffer . . . worrying if you knew or not!"

"There's no need for dramatics." Mom laughed. "I was sure you'd tell me when you were ready," she said. "And you might as well know that your guidance counselor called me about the suspension meeting on Monday."

I fell back on the couch. "Oh no," I moaned. "You knew about that too?"

Mom put on one of her "Maggie" looks. "You *know* mothers find out everything! And when a mother is also a teacher, what chance have you got?"

"But why didn't you tell me?"

"Just because." She walked over to the window and

stared out, and I wondered what was coming next. Finally she said, "At first I waited for you to tell me, and I was really angry when you didn't. And I was angry that you were in trouble; you've always been such a good kid. Then I realized that I've taken that for granted all these years — you and Maggie being good kids, I mean."

"I'm not so great," I muttered.

When Mom turned around her eyes were wet, but she was smiling. "Anyway, I didn't say anything because I got you into this. I'm really sorry that you were hurt because of my decision to use my book in school. I shouldn't have done that. It wasn't fair. I should have. . . ."

I leaped up. "Aw no, Mom. You've got to do what's right. Isn't that what this whole Crusade has been about, doing what you think is right? And Gram and Maggie and me, we're with you all the way."

For that I got another hug.

"Enough! I've got to go." I grabbed my swim bag and escaped. "See you at the meet!" I called as I ran out the door.

17

I was kind of glad Buzz wasn't with me because his idea of warming up is to goof around and be real loose. But I like to shut out the world. It starts when I get a whiff of the chlorine, and then I can think myself through the events. Once I even pretended I was getting a gold medal at the Olympics, and that day I set a school record.

Sikorski came up behind me on the way into school. "How're you doing, Troy? Some rally, huh? We going to win tonight?"

"Are you kidding? We're going to make Riverdale look like they're floating on waterwings." The adrenaline was building already. I could feel the charge of power surging.

Sikorski pulled open the door and in the hall light he saw my eye. "Wow, what a shiner." He shook his head. "Hey, I'll see you in a minute, it's my turn to check the towels."

That was okay with me. I wanted to be alone as long as I could. I pulled open the locker room door and headed for the last locker in line in the far left corner. But just as I turned down that aisle I tripped over someone's long legs sticking out. I fell against a metal locker and smacked my sore eye again.

When I pulled myself together I saw Baxter folding his long legs in under the bench. "Get out of my way," I said.

"Sorry," he muttered. "You okay?"

"Yeah, I'm okay, no thanks to you. Get out of here."

Baxter stood up slowly until I was looking at his shoulder. He grabbed my jacket. "Look, squirt, I said I was sorry. And there's nothing I can do to put last night right. So bug off. If you got any more to say, say it now."

I had plenty more to say, but a big hand clamped down on my shoulder. "No more of that, you hear?" It was the coach. "I saw the scuffle last night," he said, "but it's over now, you understand? Over. We're a team. We work together. I don't care how you feel about each other outside this locker room, but here you're buddies. On your feet, Baxter, Troy. I want you to shake hands."

So we shook hands, as though we had a choice, right?

"That's better." The coach sounded like we'd signed some major truce, and he marched back to his office.

I was pulling my sweatshirt over my head when I heard Baxter say something, but I didn't pay any attention. So he came closer, and let himself down on the bench next to me like a bag of bones. "I'm sorry your grandma got hurt."

"Sure, now leave me alone."

"Troy, you're really dim. My mother's right about you. You're just a jock. You got a head like a block. You don't think."

"Me? How about you? Trotting off after your mommy like that." All that adrenaline I'd been building up for the swim meet felt like it was going to burst out in a fast fist to Eddie's face. What was happening to me? It was just like

· 130 ·

I'd told Mom; everytime I saw this guy I felt like fighting.

"Haw! Man, that is good, you know that? Me follow my mother around? Give me a break. You're so wound up in what your mother does you can't think of anything else." Baxter turned and slammed his fist into a locker. He grunted. "What's the matter with me? Every time I see you I want to smash you."

I sat down. My arms were still in the shirt that was dangling between my knees. I looked at Eddie. "Say that again."

"I want to smash you!"

"No, what you said before that."

"That you couldn't think of anything except your mother?" Eddie asked.

"Yeah. Funny thing for you to say. Every time your mother gets off on some new committee, you get all hot about it, too."

Eddie shook his head. "It's like that cop said. You think you got your mother all figured out and she pulls something new on you every time. Funny folks, mothers." He ambled toward his locker, and started to get undressed. A couple minutes later I would have sworn he was crying, just a little. His shoulders shook. He spun around. He was laughing! "Man, my mother was mad. Did you see her fling those books?"

"Yeah. She's got a real arm. And how about my mother and all those signs she had me packing in there? And my grandma? I couldn't believe how she flew into that crowd."

"That's some shiny eye you got," Eddie said.

"Your cheek looks like a truck drove over it."

"Feels like it parked on my lip." He touched it gently. "I thought I was a goner when I fell into that mob. Everybody was pummeling anything they could get their hands on."

We were laughing when Chang stomped into the locker room. He looked like someone had dragged him out of a hearse. "What's so funny?" he hollered. "The old man grounded me. I've got to go home right after the meet. I'm lucky he's letting me swim."

That made Baxter and me about fall on the floor. "It's not funny," Chang shouted.

"What'd you do? Miss your curfew?" Eddie asked him.

Chang didn't crack a smile. "Just about. Dad wouldn't let me go to the rally, but I did anyway. And with my luck, who did I run into when the fighting started? My dad, that's who."

That broke us up even more, and we were still gasping for breath a few minutes later when Buzz made his big entrance. By then the locker room was crammed with guys changing into suits. The door flew open and Buzz leaped up on a bench with his arms spread wide. "Ta da!" he yelled, and whipped off his ratty old ski hat.

He was bald! Like a bowling ball.

"What the . . . ?" I didn't believe this. Buzz was always telling us he was going to shave his head because hair slows you down in the water. But his mother would never let him do it.

"What the heck happened?" I asked him. "Does your mother know?"

"I'll say she knows. She *did* it!"

"She shaved your head?"

"Hey, it was that or live with my hair glued together. I told you I landed in a mess of tar. But what the heck, this'll take a couple tenths off my time, right? I'm aerodynamically perfect!"

Coach Huntley came in then to give us a pep talk and his eyes almost fell out. He started to say something, but all he could do was look from Buzz's bald head to my black eye to Baxter's cut lip and gravel-track cheeks. He shook his head and went out mumbling something about a bunch of misfits.

Buzz took over. "All right you guys. We're good! Let me hear it."

"We're good!" we hollered back.

"I can't hear you," Buzz screamed just like the coach. "The best!"

"The best," we yelled, and we charged after Buzz, out of the locker room, and down the stairs to the pool.

The bleachers were jammed already and when we hit the deck the cheers ricocheted off the tile walls. We lined up on the bench and the coach came over. "Are you boys all right?" he asked Buzz and Eddie and me.

"Couldn't be better," Eddie told him.

"Yeah, I'm gonna fly like an eagle tonight," Buzz said.

"And you, Troy? How's the eye?"

"Okay, coach, no problem."

"All right team, let's go!" He gave us a thumbs-up sign. "You can do it. You're the best."

The meet started. I was concentrating so hard on my

own event that I'd hardly noticed how fast it was going. When the 100 butterfly was called, Buzz and I peeled off our sweatpants and shirts and walked to the blocks.

"I'm going to set a record tonight," Buzz told me.

"You think so?"

"I know it."

"Not in the fly, you're not. It's mine. Tonight it's mine."

Buzz smiled. "Maybe."

We shook hands and wished each other good luck like we always do. I held my breath when the Riverdale guys came over, but it was okay. They only said good luck and we shook hands. And suddenly I realized that even if they had said something rotten about me or my mom, it wouldn't have mattered. I could handle it!

I stepped up on the block and looked out at the gallery. It was a blur of people. When the official signaled for quiet, I heard one last cheer. "Go pirate!" I'd know that voice anywhere. Mom.

I raised my arm and punched my fist high over my head. A winner's sign. With that punch I *was* the pirate. I could do anything.

"Swimmers, take your mark."

I glanced at Buzz in the lane next to me. He looked more like a buzzard than ever, crouching low, arms curved high like bony wings, and that bald head sticking out. I bent low, too, and gripped the block with my toes.

"Get set," the starter shouted.

I filled my lungs and lifted my arms straight out behind me. I crouched lower, and had the darnedest feeling that I wasn't at the school pool at all. I was balanced on the rail of the slave ship, ready to dive into the shark-infested sea. Matthew Hull to the rescue.

No. Luke Troy to the rescue!

At the crack of the starter's gun, I soared out and over the water, and I knew as sure as stars shine that this time I couldn't lose.

DATE DUE			
5/14/5 Shenise			Has
11-28-95		Billings	